THE DROWNING
and Other Stories

THE DROWNING
and Other Stories

By
Edward J. Delaney

Carnegie Mellon University Press
Pittsburgh 1999

Acknowledgements

Stories from this collection have previously appeared in the following publications: "The Drowning" in *The Atlantic Monthly*, *Best American Short Stories 1995*, and *Prize Stories: The 1995 O. Henry Awards*; "Conspiracy Buffs" in *The Atlantic Monthly*; "Notes Toward My Absolution" and "Travels With Mr. Slush" in *The Greensboro Review*; "What I Have Noticed" in *Carolina Quarterly*; "A Visit to My Uncle" in *The Crab Orchard Review*

For Kieran and Caitlin

CONTENTS

THE DROWNING

My father came from the old country in middle age and to his last he instilled in the me the peculiarities of his native tongue. Even now, at the age of seventy, I am left with his manners of speech, his inflections and growls. He left me with his sayings, and I recall one in particular, his favorite, a half-comic shout of equal parts exasperation and petition: "Forgive me, Father Alphonsus!"

Most often this was uttered in moments of high disgust. My father worked as a hod carrier until he was seventy, a job that condemned him through all those years to being eternally strong and eternally exhausted; at night, sitting in his chair in the parlor of our tenement, he would brood over the five of us, his children, as we bickered over one thing or another — the last scrap of a night's loaf, a new toy pilfered from a classmate — and he would take on the resigned look of a condemned man, and invoke the name of this priest, a man he had known long ago. And then, if my mother didn't rush from the kitchen to herd us from danger, my father would most often hit one of us.

Even late in life, he had ridged muscles along the chest and back. His face was etched with a sunburned and skeptical squint. When we were young, he hit hard. When he sat down again, walled in now by the wails of a child, he'd rub the sting from his cracked hands and fall into a black mood. "Forgive me, Father Alphonsus," he'd mumble. The meaning always seemed clear. My father was a man of weakness and vices, and he made no apologies. He prayed for strength in the face of us. Much later in life I found myself praying aloud to Father Alphonsus a time or two, such as when my own son stole a car. The matter was quietly settled in the office of a police department captain, with the victim of the theft staring at me from across the table and my son quietly sobbing. Father Alphonsus, the faceless man of grace, hovered ethereally over the proceedings.

Alphonsus, my father told us, was the most well-intentioned man he ever knew, "if such things should count for anything." Alphonsus was a near relation, the keeper of faith in Fenagh, the hamlet on Lough Ree where my father was born.

"He was a man who knew nothing but to offer the best he could," my father said. "I have neither his patience nor his benevolence." My father wasn't cruel, but he lived a life of bricks on his back, the stabbing workday sun, and day's-end liquor bought with the desire for the most liquid at the lowest negotiable rate. He'd drink and play our battered phonograph, closing his eyes and giving himself over to crackling arias. For a man who so often invoked the name of his old village priest, he found no priest here to be worthy, and he fell away from the church despite my mother's prodding. When I was seventeen and offered a scholarship to Boston College, he complained bitterly that I could do better than to deal with Jesuits, insincere bastards that they were. I suspected that my father could have done much better than his dire life, but he seemed not to want to, couldn't fully engage in the way things were. Somehow it didn't seem unusual to me that a hod carrier would prize his books, his fables and sweeping histories. He was Irish, and illegal. We could not become lace-curtain Irish, and my father would have nothing good to say about those who were. He maintained through his life the sidelong glance he learned when he had first come off the boat, before he found my mother and married her.

This Father Alphonsus was one of the few people mentioned from my father's youth. I had no sense of what this man was like, his look or manner. At times, I wondered if he was real. But one day, late in his life, my father came to feel it was desperately important to tell me a story.

This would have been 1952. My father was in his early seventies, as I am now, but he was much closer to death than I assume myself to be. A resolute smoker of filterless Camel cigarettes, he had contracted cancer of the larynx, which at the time was virtually incurable. In the nursing home, in a wicker wheelchair, he talked compulsively despite the ongoing strangulation of his voicebox. He'd take a deep breath and then release it in long rattling phrases, and I would sit and listen to it, monologues about his job and the friends and enemies and crooks and aces. Later, in his yellow-walled hospital room, he'd go on and on while I watched the rectangle of sunlight glide imperceptibly across the waxed floors and then fade and die. I sensed, in all this talk, the spiraling movement toward something central. He had, he told, me, things he needed to say. Important things. The account of Father Alphonsus's final day was one.

Alphonsus had been the youngest of six, born six weeks after his father's death by pneumonia, and from the moment of his birth his mother had unshakable plans for him. Alphonsus would be her last chance, and she was the kind of woman who felt that producing a priest was a fitting and necessary act of completion to her maternal career. From the earliest age,

Alphonsus was groomed for sacred duty. She made him tiny knitted vestments and pasteboard altars as playthings, enlisting his older brothers, rougher boys, to encourage Alphonsus to believe that he was different than themselves. Alphonsus's mother spoke to him nightly about the duties he would assume, bedtime tales about faith and good works. His oldest brother, Eamon, explained to him about celibacy, and none too charitably. The details Eamon so eagerly shared, using examples of his own sordid exploits as proof of what Alphonsus would miss, horrified the younger boy. But Eamon waited then for response. Alphonsus's nightly sessions with Mother allowed him to apply the appropriate word: sacrifice. "Good lad," said Eamon. Alphonsus, even as a child, was looking forward to the priest's solitary life. His heroes had become the Irish Hermits of the middles ages. He read stories of their lives on the rocky islands off the west Irish coast, lives of gray skies and gray seas. These stories had tones of awe, the heroism of shunning the world.

Sacrifice did not ultimately define the process of Alphonsus's rise to the priesthood. He slid through seminary and took up his works back at St. Edna's in Fenagh, his boyhood church. When his superior, the aged Father O'Donnell, passed away on the night after Christmas 1906, the twenty-six-year-old Alphonsus became his village's spiritual leader.

Nights, standing in his bedroom as rain washed the windows of the drafty stone rectory, he thought that he didn't regret what he had become, but only that he wouldn't ultimately measure up. The feeling wasn't new. He completed his studies with neither distinction nor exceptional difficulty. He never considered himself brilliant, but he had enough intelligence to also see his own utter lack of intuition. Could a priest, confronted with the fluid nature of reality, afford not to rely heavily on hunches and inspiration? In his small room in the seminary, he prayed long and searchingly, believing that the sudden feeling of enlightenment or resolve was a transmission from the Creator. But when he finished with his prayers, he felt nothing.

In the first years after ordination things went relatively well. His posting in the small village seemed clear notice that not much was expected of him from his superiors. Alphonsus presided over the reassuring cycle of dawn masses, funerals and weddings; he taught catechism and organized a football team of the younger boys. These were the things Alphonsus had imagined himself doing effectively. He'd stand at the edge of a rain-softened field, the winds off the lough making the edges of his cassock snap and tighten around his legs, and he'd watch the boys, some playing barefoot, as they kicked the ball about. He felt giant then, effecting a sternness he recalled of old O'Donnell. He hoped to instill in them the fear he'd held of the old man. But at the same time, he felt small and weak in the face of the unanticipated crisis. None had yet happened, but he knew its inevitability, if not its form. He felt that at his edges, these things could be seen by the shrewd among his parishioners: his stammering uncertainty when faced with the difficulty of a pregnant girl, Amanda Flynn, asking to be quietly married, even though half the town had already heard whispered dispatches of her condition. Or of the town's thieves and adulterers and his sheeplike acceptance of them sitting at the front pews, their faces masks of haughty and false devotion. He would meet their eyes briefly and look away.

One day, after years of this stoic service, he awakened early to a knocking on the door. This tapping was light but relentless, on and on until he had let his eyes adjust and find the phosphorescent hands of his clock. It was three o'clock. An early riser, Alphonsus was surprised to be rolled out of bed, and the insistent softness of the knocks as he descended the stairs indicated to him a call for last rites, perhaps for the elder John Flanagan, who'd been kicked shoeing a horse and had not been expected to recover. At the door, he found a boy, perhaps ten years old, shivering.

"Father, you have to hear a confession," the boy said.

"Pardon?"

"A confession. You hear confessions, don't you?"

"Well, I thought you were..." Alphonsus felt a twinge of anger. "Of course I hear confessions. But I generally don't find children at my doorstep at odd hours. Now get inside here. We'll do it in the study, and it had better be good."

"It's not I who needs to," the boy said. "The person is waiting inside the church."

What was this? Alphonsus made the boy stand in the entry and ascended the stairs to change clothes. The oddity of this demanded confession made him suspicious. For a shaky moment he worried this would be a robbery. He sat at the edge of the bed, still in his underclothing, his cassock across his knees. He tried to place the boy's face. The child was not one of his footballers; the face was reminiscent of an O'Neal, of whom there were many. They were a family of beggars who lived in a beaten-down mud cottage outside the town, near the lough shore. Alphonsus heard the door below open then shut. The thought of what might be afoot — being lured out by the boy, then thrashed for his pocketwatch — made him wary. Alphonsus went to the bedroom window and looked out. The boy had gone out, and stood on the dark lawn with a man. They were shadowy forms, but he could see they were looking up at him. The man raised his arm and waved. Alphonsus waved back, then held out a raised index finger: *one moment*. The man nodded.

When Alphonsus came out the door, he felt the glassy coldness cutting through his sweater. The man and boy moved forward to meet him, in the steam from their own breathing. The man, his face hidden in the pulled-down front of his cap, was staring at the ground.

"The boy said you'd gone inside the church," Alphonsus said.

"No, Father. He's right inside the confessional."

They stayed in the yard while Alphonsus went in. He fumbled for a candle at the back of the nave, still half-waiting for hands to seize at him from the dark. But in the weak light the church was still. He entered the confessional, snuffed the candle, and slid back his screen.

"Are you there?" Alphonsus said.

"Aye, Father."

"Then go ahead."

The voice began its recitations, mumbled Latin, and as he waited Alphonsus rubbed his eyes of sleep and wondered about the elder John Flanagan and whether he'd lived through the night. Alphonsus was feeling light and electric, not quite anchored in the dark. He realized there was silence.

"Go ahead," he said.

"Father, I've breached the Fifth Commandment."

Alphonsus was silent. He was sure the man was confused. "Do you mean adultery, then?" he said.

"No."

"Tell me the Fifth Commandment."

"Thou shalt not kill."

Correct. Alphonsus felt strangely calm. This was the first time he'd encountered such an infraction. A killer! He silently recalled the seminary lessons: *Forgiveness is the priest's task, punishment the law's.*

"Who?" Alphonsus said.

"I don't know his name."

"Who knows about this?"

"No one, Father."

"Not your friends outside?"

"Not even them. Only you."

"And where is the dead man?"

"In the woods near the lough."

"Is that where you killed him?"

"That's where I did him, Father."

Alphonsus leaned back against his bench. He told himself to go slow.

"And while you were standing over his body there in the woods, were you feeling remorse for your act?"

"I felt sorry I had to breach a commandment."

"Was it self-defense?"

"In a manner of speaking."

"What manner was that?"

"That we are all in danger, Father."

"Some men, to prove their remorse, might turn themselves in."

"Aye," the voice said. "Some might."

"And why not you?"

"Others will be involved. Others who don't deserve such troubles."

"How so? Troubles from whom?"

"By the Black and Tans."

"Oh, my," Alphonsus said. He ran his fingers along the starched smoothness of his collar. Matters had taken on a more troubling dimension. He now understood that the dead man was certainly a policeman from the RIC, the Royal Irish Constabulary. It had been four years since the Irish Republican Army's Easter Rising in Dublin, and in this four years of undeclared civil war, the RICs, seen by many as agents of British rule, had more often become targets. The RICs were Irishmen, but more and more the younger men had left the ranks, some openly disavowing their ties, others simply slipping out, often to England. Those who had remained were the older hands, who after years of service were not sure whether to be more afraid of the IRA or of a lost pension. But with each new death of a constable came more recrimination and violence.

The Black and Tans, since they'd been brought in from England, had begun a policy of retribution that was as simple as it was vicious. When a policemen was killed, the 'Tans generally burned the village nearest the killing. Alphonsus did not need to calculate the distance to the shores of Lough Ree: As a sport fisherman, he knew the lough, a landlocked elbow of water a mile wide and eleven long.

"Father...?"

"Yes."

"My penance?"

Good God! Was this how simple it should be? Alphonsus was speechless. Penance? He sat for a long time, thinking, wondering in this current lack of insight whether he could somehow find the way to consult with someone. What was the penance for such an act?

"I can grant no penance yet," Alphonsus said. "I want you to return here at the same time tomorrow night. I want you to do nothing except pray. Take no action. Now, where is this body?"

"Father, I don't know if..."

"Good Lord, man! Tell me where this poor lad is so he can receive the sacrament due him!"

"Do you know the path to the rock formations on the east side of the lough?"

"I do."

"He's twenty or thirty yards north of the path, about a quarter-mile up from the shore."

"How did he get there?"

"He was answering a call for help."

The man fell silent. Alphonsus could hear his breathing. "Father?" he said.

"Father, I thought you had to grant penance."

"Not in the case of the Fifth Commandment," he said. "Most people have no experience in this." He quivered at his own lie, but his voice remained firm.

As Alphonsus sat in the confessional, listening to the receding footsteps and then the slam of the church door, he rubbed his hands on his knees, trying to calm himself. Indeed, he was thinking of the town of Balbriggen, which had burned a few weeks before at the hands of the Black and Tans.

But, Alphonsus wondered, could this man who had faced him in the confessional truly be repentant, having known what his actions would lead to? Alphonsus thought not. But he had, in his training, clear guidelines: As much as he wanted to have this man turn himself in, he could not require it. And doing so probably wouldn't help, once the dead man was discovered. The Black and Tans, so called because of their odd makeshift uniforms of khaki army trousers and black RIC tunics, were men for whom the cruelty of war had become far too ingrained. They were being paid ten shillings a day, good money, but they more often sought as payment the suffering of those they saw as enemies, which was nearly anyone Irish.

And so now there was a dead man. Alphonsus relit his candle. The movement of the shadows in the boxed closeness of the confessional made him think of the lick of flames. The Black and Tans' terror felt close at hand. Why should anyone be absolved?

In the morning, he offered sunrise service to a handful of sleepy elders and then returned to the rectory for breakfast. The housekeeper, Mrs. Toole, had brought in a two-day-old copy of *The Irish Times*, and over his toast he went through it slowly, looking for news on the Troubles. In the village, there had been talk of how the Black and Tans had taken to roaring down Dublin streets on a lorry, wildly firing their weapons; in Kiltarten, a woman was dead, hit by stray shots with a child in her arms. But in the *Times*, he found no mention.

He changed into his gardening clothes. His flowerbeds faced the woods and at the edge of the trees he had vegetables. He spent hours here, for the priesthood had not proven to be excessively demanding. Many days, he stood at his fence, watching the movements of the drawn carts and of his parishioners, the cottiers coming from the clodded potato fields. Far off, on an open meadow, unfurled bolts of linen bleached in the sun, long white bars against the hard green. Today, in the garden, he contemplated the early morning confession, and the meeting that night. It seemed to him ludicrous that he should be standing here in the garden, but at the same time he wanted to be nowhere else, for he was alone.

Down the rutted lane that curved behind the near cottages, he saw Sean Flynn, the retired schoolteacher, walking his dog. The animal, runty and of no clear breed, dug at a rabbit hole. Flynn, leaning on his cane and softly cursing the dog, saw Alphonsus, and ambled up.

"Father!"

"Mr. Flynn."

"Have we been fishing this week, Father?"

"I confess I haven't. But soon."

"Father, the weather's turning cold."

"I know, I know. It's pitiful that I haven't."

"Today, then."

"No, I have some matters."

"Father, clear your mind."

"Perhaps."

"You really should."

"I think I will, Mr. Flynn. Really."

"Today."

"Yes, today."

It would be his reason, then, to go to the lough. In the house, packing his equipment, he slipped in his stole and oils. He put on a clean cassock, and adjusted his biretta on his head, his priest's crown with its hard sides and high tassel. Mrs. Toole was down below, dusting in the dining room, and he went to the kitchen to pack a jam sandwich.

"I'll be off fishing now," he said.

"Today?" she said.

"Why not?"

"With Mr. Flanagan on his deathbed from that horse kicking him?"

"Um, well, I'll be back by mid-afternoon. I heard he's doing better."

"Really? Who told you?""

"Mr. Flynn. We were just talking outside."

Mrs. Toole went back to the dusting of the china cabinet.

"You and the fishing," she said.

"Every chance I get," Alphonsus said.

"Father?"

"Yes?"

"You're fishing dressed like that?"

"If anyone does need last rites, I don't want to do it in my fishing clothes. I shan't be long, anyway."

The row from his usual fishing spot to the shoreline edge of the path was longer than he was used to. After pulling his boat onto the rocks, he walked up and down the path several times, first making sure no one was near, then beginning to scan the thick woods for any sign of the body. The killing had been in the dark, he assumed, so perhaps the instructions were confused. The day had become brilliantly crisp, and he couldn't see anything human amidst the play of shadows and light. Alphonsus stepped off the path and walked broad circles, searching, pulling the hem of the cassock so he wouldn't get muddy. He kept his eye on the path, too, in case someone came. He wouldn't have an answer if asked what he was doing.

After an hour, he sat. He unfolded his sandwich from its greased paper and ate, thinking. He had, in his estimation, covered nearly every possible spot where a body might be. He wondered if this was a hoax. He was too exhausted and tense to fish, and the winds beyond the woods seemed to be picking up. Had he been fishing, he might have been in dangerous waters. He wished he didn't have to return to the village, to the confessional. Bad things were to happen, and he had no idea how to stop them. The body would be found by himself or someone else, or the absence of this constable would eventually become known. True as it was that some constables deserted, slipping to the north or in some cases across to Britain, it seemed to Alphonsus that only some proof of a desertion would curb the Black and Tans' impulses for destruction.

And despite his beliefs, the unwillingness to absolve the man in his confessional was stronger, a mix of revenge and principle he couldn't clearly shake free of. He didn't know if that man had been O'Neal, but he was certain it was a man like the O'Neals, embittered with his lot and perhaps too willing to blame everything on the British. But he had to absolve. So were his vows. When his sandwich was gone, he walked down to the lough and drank at water's edge from cupped hands. Back up the path, but now not as far from shore, he plunged into the wood, again searching.

The body was half-hidden with wet leaves, the accumulation on the windward side like a pyramid disappearing in the dunes. Close up, Alphonsus knelt and put his hand on the shoulder and gently rolled the man on his back.

"Hello, Thomas," Alphonsus said.

It hadn't occurred to him he'd know the deceased. It was Thomas Shanahan, a royal constable stationed at the RIC barracks on the other side of the lough. Thomas had, from time to time, come to mass at Alphonsus's church. Alphonsus had made a point to welcome him, for he believed that all were equal in the eyes of God. Thomas was also a fisherman, and after mass they had often talked of their favorite spots. Thomas's face was clean, his clothes neatly straight. He wasn't in uniform, but in thick wool trousers and shirt, as if off duty. Alphonsus turned him again, and now saw the crust of hardened blood on the back of his head. As he removed his oils and stole from his fishing kit, Alphonsus scanned the trees, ready to become prone should he hear footsteps.

Thomas was middle aged, a bachelor who, Alphonsus sensed, was as private a person as he. Thomas lived in the RIC barracks several miles to the north of Fenagh, but in his conversations with Alphonsus never spoke of any of his mates. But of course one couldn't, in the same way that Alphonsus understood there could be no mention of the Black and Tans and their tactics. Alphonsus, as he daubed the oils upon the cold face, assumed Thomas had deplored all this, and Alphonsus didn't care to know different.

When he finished the last rites, Alphonsus sat for some time on a rock, looking at the body. How had he come here? Had he been ambushed fishing? No rod or kit lay nearby, but those might have been spoils for the killer. He could go on speculating, but there was still no getting around what he now planned to do. From his own bag Alphonsus extracted his trowel, the best he had been able to manage without being noticed. He walked in a circle around Thomas, looking for the softest and highest ground, and then knelt and began digging.

This act, he knew, had transformed him. He had no business doing this. The dirt did not give as easily as he'd imagined; he'd felt, coming out in the boat, that he could be back at the rectory by dusk. But the soil was choked with rocks. Hours into it, he stood back and looked at the pitiful rut he'd clawed out, and he laughed in despair.

"Tommy," he said to the body. "I damned well don't know what to do with you. This just isn't Christian, is it?" Tommy, on his side, stared out onto the lough.

Alphonsus peered up through the trees, not able to shed the

sense he was being watched. He had the feeling that the killer might come back, to see the body still there. The IRA wanted the body to be found, surely, to ensure that a bloody raid by the 'Tans was inevitable. The killing of a fellow Irishman like Tommy would create doubt and ambivalence unless there was the necessary retribution by the Brits. Was he being used in this? Was there an expectation that Alphonsus himself was going to report the death? Or would they return, having thought things over, to put Tommy in a more conspicuous place?

His plan had been to bury Tommy, but Alphonsus now saw he wasn't capable of finishing the job. The hole was barely two feet deep. Alphonsus recalled his grandfather's stories of the Famine, of skeletal men burying cloth-shrouded friends as packs of starving dogs gathered at the periphery, yelping with hunger and bloodlust, set to dig as soon as the living moved on.

"Forgive me, Tommy, but I can barely move now," Alphonsus said. "I thought my gardening had made me fit enough to undertake this."

A wind was picking up on the lough, making the water choppy and whitecapped. The row back would be dangerous if he didn't go soon. He felt a rising panic. He would have to drop Tommy into the deep waters — he saw this. He'd not be back until well after dark, but his midnight confession awaited. He'd have to be there or the killer would certainly have suspicions.

Down by the water, he searched for a way to weight down the body. Rocks were all around, but no means of attachment. His fishing kit could be loaded, but the top was loose and presented the strong chance that the ballast would fall out as the package sank. Alphonsus saw one way to do this. Standing above the body, he removed his cassock, and then pulled off Thomas's pants and shirt.

Getting the cassock onto the body was easy. Thomas was a bigger man than he, but the cassock was loose. Alphonsus adjusted the braces of Thomas's pants and rolled up the pants and shirt cuffs so that he was clothed for the stealthy trip back to the rectory. In the pocket was a purse with Thomas's papers and a sizeable bit of money. Alphonsus was surprised that this hadn't been taken.

The boat rode low on the water with two men in it, the dead one loaded down with stones, the live one weighted by the terror of being caught. Alphonsus had used his fishing line to bind the bottom of the cassock around Thomas's ankles to hold the rocks; the collar was snug at the neck. The last trace of sunlight was nearly gone. Alphonsus stroked hard against the winds, slicing out toward the rough middle of the lough.

He was a sinner now — he could see that. He would dump a dead man into the cold waters as if a load of garbage, would grant penance to a murderer. He would return to his rectory, slip past Mrs. Toole so she wouldn't notice his inexplicable change of clothing, and he would spend the rest of his life trying to live with this. And all he wanted was for no one to be hurt. So be it. If this body somehow resurfaced or washed to shore, with a cracked skull and wrapped in a cassock, so be it. Or if the 'Tans correctly interpreted Tommy Shanahan's disappearance and overran Fenagh anyway, so be it. "So be it, Tom," Alphonsus said. "A week will pass and you won't turn up, and they'll know, they'll know."

He stopped rowing. The moon shone through a break in the clouds, giving definition to the far edges of the lough. To say a prayer at a moment like this seemed crude and sacrilegious, desperate and artificial. But he prayed now anyway, prayed for guidance.

Nothing came to him. He felt that matters were on an inevi-table course, and there was nothing to do but to send Tommy to the bottom and then to go home. "Do as we must do," he said to the body.

He grabbed the shoulders of the cassock. He crouched in the boat, the balance becoming slippery, and then he lurched and Tom hit the gunwale. The boat was listing. Water was pouring in. He had imagined a noiseless taking of the body, but now Alphonsus was in a fight, and in his panic he wasn't sure whether he was trying to shove the body away or pull it back on board. But neither was happening and now he was underwater, the coldness and dark shockingly sudden. He looked up and could see only a single blurred spot of weak light. He wanted to reach for it, that moon in the sky over on the other side of the surface. His hands were still clenched to the bunched fabric of his own cassock, now weighted with death, and he let go of it, and that solid block that was Thomas grazed his leg and ankle and then was gone.

Alphonsus had been hanging onto the side of the overturned boat for hours when he decided he would not return to Fenagh. That he would survive was not a given; the water was cold enough and his arms were tired enough from the digging that he felt almost nothing, except for the dull pain of the thick muscles along the neck. But he clung on, the wind and waves rocking him in crests and swells until he was desperate enough to push away from the boat and swim for shore.

His thought, as he crawled out of the water on his hands and knees, was still of his hat, his black biretta, floating like an ornate ship far out of reach, its black pompom now a keel. He had seen it from the boat, puffed by the wind and etched by moonlight, unwilling to sink with the cassock. The boat, too, would be found, far off on the lough, known by those fishermen who knew him.

In the woods, he undressed, squeezed water from his clothing. He considered trying to light a fire. Naked in the cold air, he plunged again in the water to clean himself, and then dressed in the wet woolen shirt and trousers. His black brogans squished loudly when he walked, but he was moving quickly. In no time he was well up the path and along the rutted highway toward Dublin. By dawn he would find a ride in a chicken lorry, and by that evening he would use Tommy Shanahan's wet money to get a room over a public house by the docks. Three days later, his clothes dry and black stubble making his face lose its delicacy of appearance, he would use the remaining money to bribe a dockworker to get him into the steerage of the first ship leaving Ireland. It would happen to be going to Boston. The dockworker would ask, "Why are you going?" The answer would be this: That the stowaway was a Royal Constable from near Fenagh, that he was running away, and that he hoped no one would find out; and when these words were out, the dockworker's face was so twisted with revulsion that there was no question that this would be common knowledge in Fenagh in a few day's time.

My father, telling this story thirty-two years later in a wheel-chair in the rest home where he would die, told me that this is how he came to be a man born in middle age, with a name picked from a city directory. He told me he felt the need to unburden himself, that my mother never knew, and that he was for that reason glad she had preceded him into death. He said this without a hint of expectation that I would say any-thing to console him, and I didn't. I couldn't. I was in my twen-ties then, leaning over the man who had hit me so hard and so frequently that I had gone to bed many nights wishing to be someone else, a different child. I should have said something. But I stared at him until a nurse came to us and said he needed to eat.

A few years ago, I went to Ireland, for the simple reason that

I am a devout Boston College football fan, and that year they played an exhibition game in Dublin against West Point. I boarded an Aer Lingus 747 packed with alumni, and we sang drinking songs high over the Atlantic. It was only in the day after the football game that it occurred to me to rent a car and take a drive. Asking in Dublin, I found no one who'd heard of Fenagh, but I set out toward Lough Ree and on its eastern shore I got directions to the town. There, I parked, and walked the length of its primary streets, and stood for a while in front of St. Edna's Church, without going in. At a small shop, I talked to the keeper, a man older than me, and he told me he had a niece in Boston he sometimes went to visit. I told him I'd had a relative here, a Father Alphonsus.

"Of course," he said. "I've seen the plaque." He pointed me down the road toward a knoll overlooking the water. There, behind some overgrown brambles, I found an engraved plate, the size of an envelope maybe, mounted on a rock.

"Father Alphonsus Kelly, RIP. Drowned November 5, 1920."

I stood on the knoll and looked at the harsh waters where this man had lost his life and become someone else. He was a man who became old and could not aspire to the better part of himself he believed he had squandered who had come to find, I think, that in his exile that he couldn't bring himself to try to be like Alphonsus, who indeed was a specter that floated over all our lives. Standing at the edge of the lough, I said a prayer for my father. I petitioned that he might be delivered, from a purgatory of which I had been part.

HERO

In 1976, the summer after my sophomore year of high school, my uncle hired me to be a bar boy at the Ancient Order of Hibernians lodge, where he had tended bar every Thursday, Friday and Saturday night since he got home from the Second World War. Days, he was a freelance electrician. But it seemed that for as long as I could recall, his beat-up Econoline panel truck mostly stayed in the driveway of our house, which he owned. He had the first floor, renters had the second, and my mother, little brother and I lived in the two-bedroom up under the eaves.

My mother was my uncle's kid sister, which you could pretty much tell. My father was long gone, and my uncle, Chuck, looked after us. I had figured out that he didn't even charge us rent for our apartment. When the time came that I needed stuff — clothes, going-out money, whatever — my uncle said I could wash glasses for him, and I think now that it was also a way of keeping me occupied weekend nights, and therefore out of trouble.

I didn't mind. I didn't have as much to do with my time as Uncle Chuck thought I did. The AOH was a block down from the house, and in the neighborhood, mostly wooden triple-deckers, the windowless stone building with "Hibernia" carved over the archway door seemed as forbidden a place as any I knew. It was a place where men disappeared from their wives, a secret clubhouse not much different from the one my brother and I had once made out of a refrigerator box in the damp cellar of our house. My uncle wore a maroon golf shirt with "AOH" embroidered over the heart. That I was legally too young to be in there was a powerful draw. I immediately accepted the job.

The bar itself was in the basement, and with the exception of membership meetings and special functions up in the main hall, it was the only part of the building that was ever open. It was paneled in knotty pine with a checkerboard linoleum floor and a jukebox people mostly didn't play, and two pool tables with netted leather pockets that stood in the hung light of a couple of bare fluorescent tubes.

Uncle Chuck ran the place, which included overseeing gambling pools and the repayment of small loans from the cash box. This was part of the deal, he said, because these men who came to drink were more than friends. "They're my brothers, Peter," he said to me. "We take care of them no matter what."

Taking care of them meant that part of my job, a big part of it, was walking drunken men home and making sure their wives got them inside the door. I was big for my age, and could have carried the smaller men if I wanted to, but I had to admit that as I did this, as these men leaned their weight against me and trusted my strength and thanked me again and again for my damned kind assistance, I could see how they took it as something shared among friends, something not to be ashamed of. If they were not so drunk as to be incoherent, they tipped me, usually a dollar. Once in a while, a sloppily grateful customer (after wrestling out of my helping grip during the actual walk) would shove a ten or a twenty at me. Anything over twenty, and I had to bring the money to Uncle Chuck, who would put it in an envelope with the man's name on it , in escrow for when that man came back worried that he had misplaced a fifty or even a C.

Most of the people who came to the AOH were veterans. Most had been in the same war as my uncle, and some had been in Korea, and only a few in Vietnam. The guys who had been in Vietnam were just a few years out of it, most of them still in their early twenties; they were quieter, guys who came here because the clubs people their age went to were too noisy, too jangling. They were mostly guys working construction or in trades, brought in by the older men. The AOH was a place for heavy, quiet drinking.

Flick O'Neill was the guy people said was a hero. Some men my uncle's age had apparently done heroic things, but that was thirty years past, and seemingly irrelevant. Flick, a bearish guy with scrubby long hair and sideburns that kind of faded into a three-day growth, was notable in the freshness of his deeds, whatever they might have been. Indeed, Flick barely seemed older than me. He'd gone into the service on his eighteenth birthday and was still, five years later, not past the look of a teen-ager.

I didn't know exactly what it was he had done. Other people seemed to know, but I wasn't given the time to hear it out. In my job, I danced along the rubber mat behind the bar, soaping glass and clearing the bartop while Uncle Chuck drew beer and bantered with the customers. I rarely tried to talk with anybody, and when I did it rarely seemed to work out. One night, I passed by Flick, who was sitting with another guy his age, and I said to him, "Why do they call you that?"

He looked at me, then his friend, and he said, "Because I like to go to the movies," and his friend snorted. Flick just looked into his drink, and I abandoned any further efforts in that direction.

———

At the AOH, nobody really talked about the war, the way nobody talked about the war anywhere in those days. It was only a year after it had ended, and it seemed then people still didn't want to believe we lost but were pretty much beginning to know it. Nobody seemed up for reminiscing the way they constantly did about the Good War, about Saipan and Anzio. The snippets of Vietnam stories you did hear were gruesome, different and more scary than the clean tales my uncle's friends liked to tell. My uncle allowed that Flick had been a Navy Seal. I pictured darkly clad men moving with a river tide, cloaked in night. You didn't hear much about Seals then, and my uncle kept saying that the things Flick did were "highly covert," and that was part of the reason Flick apparently had no medals — that his exploits had been too secret to even acknowledge. I wasn't always sure I believed that, but I was interested.

Flick mostly wore jeans and work shirts. He looked like a construction worker but as far as I knew he didn't work. His hair was long and halfway greasy, and he was almost always in on Fridays and Saturdays, sometimes shaven, sometimes not. He had a round baby face that seemed startling when unbearded. He looked meaner with a growth, and I think he liked looking mean. When someone put on the jukebox, a sporadic event there, he'd turn and glare, and stop talking until the song was over.

Flick's father sometimes came with him. His name was Johnny O'Neill, and he made up for Flick's reticence. Johnny had fought in no war as far as I could tell, and he was a happy soul. He'd make jokes at everyone's expense and nobody seemed to mind, especially because he bought enough drinks to grease any anger. Everybody called him Johnny, even me, and he told me that I must be some kind of a hot shit to get a job at the

AOH before I was even old enough to be in the place.

On nights the Red Sox were on the old Motorola that hung on a shelf over the bar, Johnny O'Neill would get serious and wild. He hated Jim Rice, the Sox's prized left fielder, for reasons hard to figure. The Sox had just been to the World Series, but as far as it concerned Rice, Johnny didn't want to hear about it. His eyes would burn when Rice came to bat, and he would sit there on his stool, muttering and cursing while Rice slowly dug in to face the pitch. "Hurry up, you goddamned shine," Johnny would sputter, and around him, the others would giggle and egg him on. "Goddamn bonehead," Johnny would spit.

It had been a funny summer in that way. Usually, things in the neighborhood were pretty much Live and Let Live, but now there was all this talk about busing black kids into our school. People didn't like it, didn't think it was fair to force outsiders on us, and were getting angry. Uncle Chuck didn't seem to disapprove of this view, but I knew my mother would have. She was proud to be different. She told me that she and myself and my brother weren't just neighborhood types, we weren't townies, but she said it in a half-sly way that intimated that this was a secret.

My mother had been elsewhere. I had been born in Florida, before my father, who was not one of us, evaporated. We came back up, to be looked after by Uncle Chuck and his wife, Edna. That I had an Italian surname in the neighborhood had made me stick out, and Uncle Chuck finally asked why the hell we all just didn't go back to Geary, which we really were, after all. My brother Jason, who was four years younger, didn't much care. I didn't, either. Or if I did, I was glad to be able to melt into the rest of it, without exactly lying. One Friday after school, Uncle Chuck took my mother and brother and I to see a judge, and it was done. Coming out, I wasn't sure if I felt the change.

Flick O'Neill rarely missed a Friday night at the AOH. Some nights, he'd shoot pool with Johnny, spreading quarters along the bumper in a way that nobody challenged him; in those long unhurried games he'd rarely speak, even as Johnny goaded him by criticizing his shots and joking about his bad form.

"Where the hell did anybody teach you to play pool?" Johnny said while Flick ignored him. "They sure as hell didn't teach you to shoot pool in the service. What the hell did they teach you, anyway?"

"How to kill a man twenty-eight ways," Flick finally said.

"Well they should've held it down to twenty-five ways, and then taught you to play pool," Johnny said.

"I play pool fine," Flick said.

"You play like crap," Johnny said, smiling so that his cigarette was clamped between his teeth. "There are basic things a man has to master."

I saw most of these men outside the AOH, in their daytime guises. Cheney, who sometimes drank so much he laid on the pool table to rest, even if a game was going on, was our mailman; Shea, who owned the seat at the corner where the bar curved toward the wall, was a counterman at the diner near the high school. Here and there, I saw faces I knew from the AOH, even a few cops like Mr. Conlan, who was a Boston Police detective.

But I never saw Flick around the neighborhood, and the exotic nature of his secret background made it like he really wasn't from here. And the truth was, the only time I ever saw Flick outside the AOH was far from home.

My mother wanted me to be a young gentleman. For my school clothes, she sent me to a shop across Mass Avenue from Harvard Yard. The clothes were nice enough, but it seemed like my mother sent me with the idea these clothes would cloak me in something that had the faint scent of higher stations, of higher mindedness. She was working then as a typist for Boston Edison, and I knew that she had to make the room to afford the clothes, and I respected that.

Maybe twice a year, I took the subway over to Cambridge. It was, for me, an event. The seedy circus that presented itself around the old kiosk was bohemian in a way that excited me, with the street musicians and the three-card-monty types and the vaguely spacy students. It was hotly antithetical to the neighborhood, and its timeworn ways. The air was always slightly suggestive of contraband, and I would sit on a wall pretending I was older and watching the college girls go by. It was not to say I felt in any way part of it. I had come to feel, early on, like the abiding observer, and I didn't fool myself into thinking that anyone looking at me thought I belonged.

That day I saw Flick, my chest got tight with excitement. There he was, with an Army-surplus coat on and a red headband, and with him — clearly with him — was a girl, and this girl was black.

They were obviously involved. They weren't exactly touching, although her hand was sort of brushing along his thick thigh. It was the way they were joined, by looks and whispery talk and sly smiles. She looked a little older than him, maybe in her middle twenties, and her clothes were like his — army coat, threadbare jeans, cheap sneakers. She had her hair in a perfect Afro, as wide as a halo and perfectly arranged. She was wearing shades, big round lenses, and every so often, he'd reach over and try to lift them, and she'd push his hand away with a shy half-grin. And here they were, in a place where no one seemed to even notice, except me.

I kept looking, shocked and ashamed of my shock. My mother would have said that I was showing my biases, just by looking. But I couldn't look away, locked in like it was an eclipse of the sun I couldn't stop staring at, even as it burned my eyes. For a moment, Flick looked up. I was at least a hundred feet away, and amid the swirl of the crowd I would have been hard to spot. It seemed that he ignored me so steadfastly at the AOH I thought he might not recognize me. But it seemed for a moment that our eyes locked. We were far enough apart that it seemed that way but could have been the illusion. But then the girl said something, and he sort of laughed, and he looked back to her.

The next Thursday, when Flick came into the AOH, he sat in front of where I stood, glanced across the bar at me, then asked Uncle Chuck for a beer. If we had made a connection, he wasn't showing it, and I could respect that. He suddenly seemed braver and more admirable. He seemed even more elevated — the risk he was taking, the contrariness of all that. I didn't really care if he was truly in love with the woman, it was that element of danger in being out in the open, doing something that just wasn't done in the Neighborhood. All around him, my uncle and his friends and customers — an entirely different generation of men — carried on their usual way, and I could see more clearly now the image of Flick crawling on his belly on a jungle floor, in a different country, unafraid.

"How you doing, Flick?" I said, and he didn't answer. But it was the indifference of his non-answer that made me realize he hadn't seen me at all.

Our apartment at the top of Uncle Chuck's house looked like it was decorated for a quick escape. We had a basic set of furniture (secondhand sectional sofa, five-piece dinette, mattresses on boxsprings set on the floor). We had nothing on the walls, nothing that seemed to personalize the place. My mother's influence, that of quiet resistance, hung throughout our small space. It didn't matter, because we never invited anyone in.

Uncle Chuck said she had a contrary personality, and that

this had driven her to do foolish things. He saw her as immature. He worried about whom she was insulting at her job over at Boston Edison. Then she'd ask him what he meant by that.

"You and your way-out ideas," he'd say.

Sometimes she'd ignore him, and sometimes she'd take him on. One night, he had come up to drop off a package, a paper bag he had under his arm. My mother was sitting on the arm of the sofa, brushing her hair. She had just come out of the shower, and was by the open window trying to get the hair dry, which was tough in the summer because of the humidity and because she hadn't cut it since we'd come back from Florida. It hung past her waist. The conversation had started with the hair, in fact; Chuck wondered if they objected down at her office.

"Why would they?" she said.

"You look like a kid, with the hair so long," he said.

"For God's sake, Chuck, I'm thirty-four years old," she said.

"That's not so young," he said. "You can't live like a kid forever. You act like what I say is so old-fashioned."

"Chuck," she said, "I'm not ready to throw in the towel yet."

"I'm saying take some responsibility," he said. "It wouldn't hurt you to think about maybe getting married."

"Oh, God!" she said. "To who ? One of your townie friends?"

"Hey, you're a townie, too," Chuck said. "Whether you like it or not."

She didn't answer him then. She turned away from him and bent over the open screenless window, hanging her hair out to try to get a breeze on it.

Uncle Chuck looked at me. I was sitting on the other end of the sofa, watching our little black-and-white.

"Hey," he said, pulling the paper bag out from under his arm like he'd forgotten about it. "Look what I have here." He reached inside, and pulled out a shirt, which he held up for me to see. It was a maroon golf shirt with "AOH" embroidered over the heart, like his own but in my size.

The next Saturday, I counted out my bar money and took the subway back over to Harvard Square. I didn't know whether I was hoping to see Flick, or whether having seen him like that had made me see this place as exciting and dangerous. I had enough money in my pocket that I could sit on the sidewalk drinking soda and throwing coins into the open guitar case of a man who stood through the afternoon singing folk tunes. I must have put five dollars of quarters in across that afternoon, and he finally seemed to notice.

"You're supporting me here," he said, grinning. "You like Woody Guthrie? I play Arlo, too."

"I just like hanging around, listening," I said.

"Good enough," he said. "Good enough. You stay all you want. You've paid enough that you can even make requests, if you want. Okay, Slim? What's your name, Slim?"

"My name is Peter," I said. "Peter Giannini." I hadn't really thought about saying that. It had more or less just come out. I had been Pete Geary for two years now. I knew if Uncle Chuck had ever heard that, he'd have been none too pleased.

That night, I went back to work. When I came in, Uncle Chuck eyed me as I put on my apron.

"The shirt fits good," he said.

"Thanks," I said, looking down at it.

"Where the hell have you been all day?" he said.

"Just knocking around," I said. "Nowhere special."

"I was looking all over. I needed to move the old TV out of here." He pointed up. A new color television hung on the shelf in the corner.

"Wow," I said. "Where did that come from?"

"The kitty," he said. "I've been putting small change in a jar, for about two damned years. People wanted a better TV. The

Sox are on against the A's tonight. My back's killing me from doing it myself."

"Sorry," I said.

"So where were you, anyway?"

"Just knocking around," I said, and he looked at me for a little longer, then turned and went to wash some glasses.

That night, maybe because of the new TV, people crowded in at the bar. The game was in Oakland, so it didn't even start until ten o'clock, but the bar was open until one and would stay open if the game wasn't over by then. It was a good match, and Uncle Chuck took out a small spiral notebook from under the bar and walked along the length of the place, taking bets and putting bills under the elastic band he had strung around the notebook. Nobody wanted Oakland, even though they had Vida Blue pitching. Uncle Chuck had to push the odds to ten-to-one, just to get people to wager. When he was done, he walked back behind the bar, where I was drawing a pitcher for Detective Conlan. Uncle Chuck went to put the notebook away, noticed me, and said, "Well? You want to bet?"

"I'll take Oakland," I said, handing him three crumpled ones, and Conlan eyed me distrustfully. "Hey, somebody's got to even the sides," I said, and he walked away with his pitcher, shaking his head.

Johnny and Flick O'Neill were at the seats directly under the television.

"Beats the tube you got at home, huh?" Uncle Chuck said.

"Damned right it does," Johnny said. "Because I don't even have a damned TV. There's not a goddamned thing to watch on TV anymore."

"Except the Sox," I said.

"The Sox are a bunch of friggin losers," he said, staring at the screen.

After Hobson, Lynn, Yastrzemski and Fisk went down, Rice came up in the top of the second.

"Here comes the shine," Johnny said. "Here's the big tough man."

"Pop, the guy's second in the league in home runs," Flick said.

Johnny looked at him as if he were a stranger. "No shit that he is," he said. "Watch what's about to happen. His buddy Blue there is about to serve up a nice fat pitch. That's what they do. They take it easy on each other."

"What?" Flick said, grinning incredulously. "What are you saying? That Blue's gonna let him hit because he's black?"

"They do it, Stupid," Johnny said.

"You wish," Flick said.

"What I'm saying is true," Johnny said more quietly, sipping the suds of his beer, and I could hear some of the others beginning to chuckle.

"That's ridiculous," I said.

Both Flick and Johnny turned to me as if they'd just noticed I was alive. I looked to Flick, since I had been in agreement with him. He said, "Why don't you shut the hell up?"

I did. People acted like they weren't listening, and I heard the announcer describe Rice taking the first pitch for a ball.

"Get back to work," Uncle Chuck said, loudly enough for people to hear. "And quit bothering the customers."

He didn't say anything else the rest of the night. The next morning, when he came up to install a light fixture in my mother's closet, Uncle Chuck said, "There's no point in tangling with customers over that kind of thing."

He had me stand beside the stepladder, handing up tools.

"Don't get on Johnny's bad side," Uncle Chuck said, his head up against the closet ceiling. "He just shoots his mouth, but he's a basically decent guy. And you're not supposed to even be in the place, and it's the money of guys like Johnny that support you."

"I just sort of said it," I said. "I didn't really think ahead."

"I know that," he said. "Forget about it, but just don't do it again."

"But what he said was really ridiculous," I said. "You have to admit it."

"Yeah, I suppose it was," he said. "Johnny isn't too fond of the colored."

"And it's just way out of line, using words like that," I said. "They want to be called 'black.'"

He brought the screwdriver down, and I took it, and he leaned down to see which tool it was he wanted. "What should you care?" my uncle said, looking at me.

"I just do," I said.

"All right, already," he said.

It was late that summer that my mother started talking about moving. She started mentioning Florida, but she'd talk about Arizona, too, and Los Angeles.

"It's like I can only go so long around here without getting the itch," she said. "Don't you want to see another part of the country, boys?"

My brother and I both said yes, but I found myself frightened. I didn't really want to go, even though I couldn't think of many reasons why we shouldn't. I wondered at times whether I'd be a lifer in the Neighborhood, like Uncle Chuck, and whether I liked that idea or not. Did I belong? Florida interested me because my father might still have been down there, and I wondered what he'd say if he found out I was now going by the name Geary. Maybe he wouldn't care one way or another, I thought.

But my mother as quickly discarded the notion of Florida and began talking more about Los Angeles. I took it to be just thinking aloud, anyway. I felt my mother could survive in the neighborhood as long as she thought of herself as being separate from it, beyond its hold. I didn't think we'd move, couldn't see how we could, without any money.

When she talked this way, I could tell it made my brother even more nervous than it made me. Jason was eleven, and he didn't remember Florida the way I did. He didn't remember our father at all. My mother was standing in the kitchen one night, kneading dough on a board for muffins, and she began describing California to us, as if she'd been there.

"There are palm trees, just like Florida," she said. "And the weather is never as hot as this. Think of the best June day, every day."

"Who would we know?" Jason said.

"We wouldn't know anybody," my mother said, as if startled from a reverie. "That's the point. It would be just the three of us, on our own. We wouldn't owe anybody."

"We wouldn't know anybody?" Jason said, and I could tell he was getting antsy. Our mother's back was to us, and I touched him on the arm and shook my head, No, to make him understand it was just talk.

I obeyed Uncle Chuck and left Johnny O'Neill alone, but Johnny wouldn't let it go. I had my hair long that summer, like just about everybody else my age, but suddenly Johnny couldn't seem to abide it.

"Oh little girl," he'd say. "I need another beer. Miss?"

I'd look at Uncle Chuck, and he would give me a sideways grin, and I'd keep my mouth shut. Flick, whose hair was longer than mine, was most often shooting pool, ignoring it all.

Some afternoons I'd go back over to Harvard Square thinking I'd see him. I didn't tell my mother I was looking for him, but I finally did tell her where I was going, and she liked the idea.

"I should go with you sometime," she said.

"No," I said. "I mean, you wouldn't like hanging around, the way I do. I just hang around."

"Well then," she said. "I'll just go myself, sometime. Maybe I'll run into you, maybe I won't. You never know who you might see when you're out."

When I went, I didn't find Flick, or the black girlfriend. I'd sit on a wall in the sunshine, wanting to see, as if it was my defiance rather than his own. But nothing ever happened. I was beginning to tire of my vigil, and one afternoon, a man in a suit followed me up Mass Avenue and then down an alley, where I was heading to take a leak. He came around just as I had started, and he watched me.

"Thirty bucks for a blow?" he said.

"No," I said. "I don't really do that."

"You don't understand," he said, smiling. "The deal would be that I give you a blow, and then I give you thirty bucks."

"No, but thanks," I said. I finished and zipped up, but I could see peripherally that he wasn't leaving. I moved toward the avenue, but he stepped sideways and blocked my way. He stuck out his hand, to shake, and I wasn't sure what he was about to try.

"No hard feelings, right?" he said. "I thought you looked, you know, that way."

"No," I said, shaking it quickly. "I just want to go now."

"Nobody's stopping you," he said.

I went straight to the subway, and riding back I couldn't bring myself to make eye contact with anybody. I was agitated and ashamed for some reason, and in my agitation I couldn't help telling Uncle Chuck about it, in selective detail, that night at the bar. When I started into it, he pulled me to the stock room, where we couldn't be heard. I gave him the basic facts.

"Where was this?" he said. "Who was this guy? Was it a guy who comes in here?"

"It wasn't in the neighborhood," I said.

"Then where in God's name did this happen, son?"

"Cambridge," I said. "I was just hanging around Cambridge."

"Cambridge, " he said. "Does your mother know you go off and hang around in Cambridge?"

"She wanted to come with me," I said.

"Jesus, Mary, and Joseph," my uncle said.

I didn't go back to Cambridge, didn't have the faintest thought of doing so. It was a situation a guy like Flick would have handled okay, but not me. I decided that familiar terrain had its advantages: I spent my days off riding my bike down to Harbor Beach, where I sometimes saw classmates I hadn't seen since school had let out. They seemed to be impressed about where I was working, but I tried not to make a big deal.

"You ought to get us some beer," Terry Logan said.

"It only comes in kegs," I said. "No bottles."

"So get us a keg," Terry said.

As we talked, Sheila Sullivan came by and sat with us, in her swimsuit and as white as powder, sunscreen caked on her like she was ready for a channel crossing. "If you get a keg of beer, I'll be there," Sheila said.

"Can't do it," I said. "My uncle would nail me."

"Chicken," Terry said. "You afraid of those guys at the AOH?"

"Yes," I said. "You should be, too. Conlan carries that gun, even when he's off-duty. And I already have Flick O'Neill pissed off at me."

"Then you're a dead man," Terry said. "Because I heard he's one tough customer."

"Isn't that the hero?" Sheila said.

"Yeah," Terry said.

"How do you know?" I said. "What was it that he did, that made him a hero?"

"I've heard it's like, really secret," Sheila said. "You know, classified."

"Do you believe that?" I said.

"Sure," Terry said. "Do you?"

"Yeah," I said. "I guess I do."

That night, my mother caught me sneaking out, on my way to meet up with Sheila and Terry. Sheila had volunteered to swipe a bottle of schnapps from her parents' liquor shelf. I came down the unlighted back entry to the house not knowing she was there, and when I came around the bend of the stairway, she said from the dark, "Peter?"

"Jesus!" I said. "What are you doing?"

"I was just having a cigarette," she said. "It's nicer outside than inside. Where are you going at this hour?"

"I was going to meet some friends," I said. "Just to hang around."

"Friends," she said, a statement. "What kind of friends do you have, Peter?"

"Just friends," I said. "School friends."

"Are they nice?"

"They're okay," I said. "They treat me well enough."

"Have you been to Cambridge lately?" my mother said.

"No," I said. "I stopped going. I pretty much just stay around here now."

"Oh," she said. "That's too bad."

"Some strange stuff goes on over there," I said.

"That's not so bad, is it?"

"Sometimes," I said. "Sometimes it is."

"Oh," my mother said, and when she lit a match for another cigarette, her face momentarily stood out from the darkness like a mask. Then she blew out the match and it was dark again.

On the beach, the three of us sat on a spread-out bedsheet and drank the schnapps. It was my first time drinking, although I would never have admitted it; they both said they'd done it before, and I wasn't sure about that, either.

"My mother caught me going out," I said.

"And she let you go?" Sheila said.

"She's like that," I said.

Sheila had been leaning toward Terry, who was pouring our shots into Dixie cups; now, in the near-dark, I could see she was interested in what I was saying.

"What else does she let you do?"

"She lets me do anything I want," I said.

"Like what?"

"Like anything," I said. "I go where I want, and do what I want. I go to Cambridge, and hang around."

"Big deal," Terry said.

"It's pretty different over there," I said.

"Oh, right," Terry said.

"If you saw the things I saw, you wouldn't say that," I said.

"Such as?"

That's when I told them about the guy in the alley. Sheila couldn't believe it. She made me repeat it, exactly what the man had said.

"That could happen anywhere," Terry said, throwing down another shot, the way they did at the AOH. "Cambridge isn't the only place that could happen. There are lots of quiffs everywhere."

"Okay," I said. "I'll tell you something else. I'll tell you something you can't repeat."

"Go ahead," Sheila said.

"Promise me," I said to her.

She touched my arm. "I promise," she said gravely.

So I told them about Flick, and the girl.

"Yuck," Sheila finally said.

"Flick would lose a lot of friends if that got out," Terry said.

"But it won't, right?" I said.

"You don't have to protect Flick," Sheila said. "If he was doing that in a public place, and you see it, you can tell anybody you want."

"But I don't want to," I said.

"Why not?" Sheila said.

"I think he deserves it," I said.

"That's not the way people around here would think," Sheila said, as if I didn't know it.

The next night, Uncle Chuck came up to the apartment, looking for my mother. We were in the kitchen, my mother washing dishes and me at the table reading the newspaper.

"What's this about California?" he said, with his hands on his hips. My mother glanced at me in a disappointed way, and I held my hands out to proclaim my innocence. I was still sick from the schnapps and didn't have the energy to argue.

"It's just talk, Chuck," she said. "Wishful thinking. We're not going anywhere," she said.

"You know you can go anywhere you want," Uncle Chuck said. "You're a grown-up woman. But it's just that I can't help you get a job there, and you wouldn't live in a place where you paid no rent. But if you want to go, I'll help you whatever way I can."

"Chuck," she said, smiling. "Chuck. It was just talk."

"Good," Uncle Chuck said. "I'd miss you too much, if you left."

One of my jobs at the AOH bar was icing the kegs before the rush began. The place only had a little walk-in cooler, and at best two kegs would fit. I'd roll a new one in, screw on the hoses that sucked the beer out to the tap, then let it run for three pitchers to take off some of the suds. Then I'd pour the beer out in the sink. Saturdays, Cheney the mailman showed up early, and would pour himself free ones from the sudsy pitchers. That afternoon, he asked if we heard what had happened to Flick O'Neill. "He's in the hospital, all beat to shit," Cheney said.

"What?" Uncle Chuck said. "What happened?"

"He got jumped," the guy said. "Three on one. Fair odds, huh?"

"Is he all right?"

"He'll live," Cheney said. "Broken jaw. Cuts. Blood all over the place, I heard."

"Bastards!" Uncle Chuck said.

"They just jumped him," the guy said. "He was walking up Atlantic Avenue, and three of them — colored — come out of nowhere and start pounding him. This was yesterday."

"Colored?" Uncle Chuck said. Then he glanced at me. "Some blacks did this?"

My chest suddenly felt tight, and for the first time since I was about nine I thought I was going to cry. How could it happen? I wanted to tell. Right then I wanted to tell them all that Flick was not a guy this should happen to — that I knew, that I had seen.

The few other people in the place were moving toward the bar, listening.

"Bastards!" said a young guy named McGough. "Chickenshit bastards. Where on Atlantic Avenue?"

"Down near the Expressway," the guy said.

"I think we ought to go find these shines," McGough said. "I think we should go discuss this with them."

Two or three guys said they were game. Then some others said if everybody else was, they were. A half-dozen had formed a loose group, and they were beginning to move toward the door. At that moment, I wasn't sure exactly what I was thinking. Flick, they did this to. I felt at that moment that I really wanted to be with them, avenging.

Then Uncle Chuck pushed by me. "What? You're telling me you think you're going to find these three?"

"We'll find who we find," McGough said. "You coming?"

"No, I'm not coming," Uncle Chuck said. "I have to watch the bar. You're not even going to find them."

"We'll find who we find," McGough said, and he looked at me. "What about you?"

I thought for a moment I would have gone. I wanted to find these guys and hurt them, for what they had done. My uncle pushed me back and stared at McGough. "What the hell's the matter with you?" he said. "This is a kid. He works here, and he's not going with you guys."

"I want to go," I said.

The way my uncle stared at me and searched my eyes told me that I had just changed in some basic way. He put his palm on my chest and he said, almost whispering, "No." He kept the palm there. "No," he said.

"Hey, whatever," McGough said. "When you go see Flick in the hospital, tell him what a couple of heroes you guys were."

I heard later that they drove around, three carloads with base-ball bats, bricks and at least one gun, but that they didn't find anybody. I saw Sheila and Terry the next day at the beach, apparently together. It was a hazy day, not quite sunny with a feel like big rain was coming, so the beach was nearly empty. When they saw me, Sheila said, "How's your friend?"

"I can't believe that happened," I said. "Of all people."

"Just goes to show," Terry said.

"It goes to show what?" I said.

"That having a girlfriend who's one of them doesn't protect you from them."

"Lower your voice," I said.

"My voice is lowered," Terry said. "Nobody knows what we're talking about anyway, except us."

Sheila said, "We haven't told anybody."

When I got home that afternoon, my mother was lying on the couch with a wet washcloth on her forehead. I thought that she must be the only person in the neighborhood who didn't know what was going on, didn't know Flick or Johnny or any of the others.

"You all right?" I said.

"Just resting," she said. "Are you past your hangover?"

"What are you talking about?" I said.

"Okay, sure," she said. "Never mind."

I sat at the end of the sofa and let her put her bare feet on my lap. "I know this guy who has a black girlfriend," I said.

"So?" she said.

"I just thought I'd mention it."

"Why should it warrant a mention?" she said. "Why must it define things?"

"Yeah," I said. I wanted to ask her what she thought. I knew she wouldn't, that this would be the game.

"Learn to look past those things," she said.

"I will," I said.

"I didn't tell Uncle Chuck about California," I said. "It must have been Jason."

"It really doesn't matter."

"I can understand when things have to be said in confidence."

"It's over and done with, Peter," she said. "You don't even have to bring it up."

———

A week or so later, when we had just opened the door of the bar and were putting down the chairs, Detective Conlan came in, wearing a suit, and he asked if the taps were running yet.

"For you, anything," Uncle Chuck said. "Going to work?"

"Straight away," Conlan said, adjusting his gun beneath his tight sportcoat.

I took a pitcher and filled a glass. He held up the glass and then drank it slowly, all in one take. He put the empty glass on the bar, contemplated it, and then said to neither one of us specifically, "You want to hear a good one?"

"Shoot," Uncle Chuck said.

"Flick O'Neill," he said.

Uncle Chuck and I looked at each other, then back at him, waiting.

"So it turns out he didn't get banged up by a bunch of strangers. Turns out he got beaten up by the brothers of his girlfriend," Conlan said, and he handed the glass to me to refill.

"Girlfriend?" my uncle said. "I thought three black guys beat him up."

"They did," Conlan said, with a vague grin. "His girlfriend's brothers. Payback. He roughed her up one time too many. This time he put her in the emergency room with a busted nose and about six other things. So they came and evened it out."

"You don't mean his girlfriend," my uncle said. "You mean a whore, or something?"

"I mean his girlfriend," Conlan said. "Flick told my guys the whole story. He told them he knew who did it, but he didn't want anything done."

"It had to be different," Uncle Chuck said.

"No, my guys know what they're talking about. She's in tough shape, Chuck. A real mess. The brothers say he was using her as a goddamned punching bag, for a long time. And I'll tell you one more thing — and if I ever heard it repeated I'd deny

I ever said it — but those three, the brothers? There's nothing wrong with those guys. They did what family has to do. Even if Flick had wanted to press charges, there's no way I would have done it. I don't respect it."

"That Flick is a strange kid," Uncle Chuck said. "It's bad business to get yourself into."

"He told the girl he loved her, but it sure didn't seem like it."

"I'll be damned," my uncle said. "He'll never be able to hold his head up in here, will he?"

"Don't think so," Conlan said. "Or Johnny."

"Johnny knows about this?"

"I don't know if he does," Conlan said. He paused and drank down the second beer. "But he will, don't you think?"

It took a week before Johnny O'Neill came in again, and when he did, you could tell it was what people had pretty much been waiting for. He went to his seat under the big color TV without mentioning anything about it; watched the Red Sox silently, drank a few beers. Jim Rice came to bat and Johnny didn't say a thing.

"Hey Johnny, Rice is up," Cheney said.

"Yeah, I see that," Johnny said. Rice grounded out, and Johnny remarked to no one in particular that he was tired and ought to get going. Nobody said anything much in return. He walked out, and that was it. I never saw him again, even on the street. He couldn't have gone anywhere, it was just that in that small crisscrossing of people the coincidence didn't present itself. I might have walked by him without noticing. I realized I had never seen him outside the AOH, so in his being driven from his stool at the end of the bar he ceased to exist for most of us. The funny part was no one asked for him, or even uttered his name. He always made the swirl of all that, but I had begun to understand that Uncle Chuck was the true center of that little society, and that he was a benevolent ruler.

Not long after that, Uncle Chuck came up to the apartment and said he didn't need me at the bar anymore. He said he'd give me money if I needed it, but I should spend more time hanging around with kids like myself.

"Okay," I said.

"If you're going to be around bad influences, at least I don't want to be the one putting you there," he said.

"Okay," I said.

I was starting school again anyway. But then the busing riots started and my mother pulled me out of there. She'd been putting away most of the money I brought home from the bar that summer, saying it was my college fund. She'd talked about that money but I'd never taken her seriously. It occurred to me much later that in those years Chuck had hopes of his own. He wanted her to save her money, but not for that. But things had gotten crazy that fall and my uncle stopped resisting. As it turned out, that money would get us to California. Things would turn out different, if not necessarily better. But that was later. As the riots went on, I stayed home and read the papers.

Flick stayed around, but I never saw him. People I knew saw him, but they were like sightings. Glimpses and rumors. The story of his beating got turned all the way around, then back again. I wanted to see him, although I had no thought to talk to him, and I even made one last ride over to Cambridge, hoping I'd run into him. The act of coming there after staying away so long made me feel like I wasn't so stupid anymore. I knew the types. I sat in different places, watching leaves blow across the brick sidewalks. When it got dark, I walked back to the subway kiosk. There had been a football game, and people walked by me with their school colors on.

I had it in my mind that if I found him I would stand up and ask him questions. I wanted to ask him if he had really hit her, and why; I wanted to ask what it actually was that had ever made him a hero, or had made people think this. But, even though there were times when I thought I'd caught a glimpse, or heard the voice, or just had that sense of him being where I could get to him, I never did find him.

O Beauty! O Truth!

I became aware of the sweetness of disobedience in the fetid classroom of a woman I will only recall as Sister Boron, purveyor of junior-year chemistry at Holy Redeemer High School. Her real nun-name escapes me now (Sister Bonaventure? Sister Boniface?) but the memory burns of a bloodless woman who hammered me with the periodic tables until I bled pure acid and finally, irretrievably, had to seek out some way to take it back at her.

I was what, sixteen? Yet the calluses were forming 'round my heart, even then. Maybe for no good reason. Those days of Sister Boron always dawned murderous, the actual academic nature of our standoffs long since irrelevant; only the incursion of her steely will, so bent on hobbling me, remains vivid. She was the medium through which I tapped a deep well of ill will. As I think of all that now, so many years later, on this final arc of reflection, I know that something must have driven her to being that way — may have even driven her into that habit, the monochrome life she led, the tight-lipped stoicism, that indifference to Earthly life: What could she have imagined as her reward?

She had the pained hunch of someone who'd been carrying

a load of shit through her life, but she was probably no more than thirty-five, the age I am now. It was hard to imagine her with a history or a future, or of movement beyond her tightly circumscribed life of orders. When she spoke of the elements, her nostrils flared, like a bull set to gore.

"Rhenium," she'd say, as no one took notes. "Atomic weight, 186.2. Atomic number 75. Discovered in 1925 by Nodack, Tacke, Berg. Hafnium. Atomic weight, 178.49..." And so on and so forth, as if she were reciting her rosary.

And then, more often than not, she would wheel: "Culhane!" she'd say at me, flecking the air with bits of moisture that had collected across her lips. "What is the atomic number of Argon?" She would lift her hand and hold it across that part of the laminated periodic chart that hung at the front of the room, as if I were that desperate to know.

Of course I wouldn't know. I never knew, except for that secret knowledge that the atomic number of Boron was 5, the atomic weight was 10.811, and that is was discovered by Gay-Lussac and Thenard. But that was the extent of things. She'd wait as if there'd be some different outcome than every other time, and I would sit silent, and she would snort at my indifference.

"Ignorance is not the path to a fruitful life, Culhane," she finally said one particular springtime day. "You are truly in quicksand...."

And, as has always been my Achilles' heel, I felt the need to respond.

"Suck it," I said, sotto voce, but knowing she'd hear. "Suck it and die." She'd stop pacing, to let me know she had indeed heard, and then after a lingering moment she'd put that right foot forward, the creak of her cumbrous shoes underlining the silence we had fallen into. She had a heavy key ring on the belt of her habit, which she liked to unclip and heft in her hand. The keyset (and I often imagined the hundred binding locks of her daily life), it must have gone a pound or two. In these moments of confrontation, Sister Boron would weigh those keys in her palm for a moment, and then move on with the lesson.

And yet, those same days had sweet counterpoint: another nun, of all. Sister Immaculata. She read us poems and some-how I acceded. She was a stumbling, birdish woman, so young beneath the furls of her habit, as if she had been sitting in our places and was forced to come up in front of us. When she read she lowered her face into the pages, muffling her voice, so that only the anxiety-slitted eyes floated above the covers, scan-ning alternately across us and the near-memory lines.

To my regret, I liked the poetry. Or at least I saw its utility. I must have felt there was something there for me. But I also knew that my main self-interest was to dispel Sister Boron's clear notion that I was not to be worked with, not teachable. Sister Boron needed to know I could be gentled, but never by her. I made sure I had laid myself at the foot of the very nun with whom the hated Boron shared her room and commuted daily from the convent. I'd seen them. I'd heard, even though those spartan Sisters of Mercy never once indulged in personal narrative, holding tight on the stories of themselves in the same way they hid their hair beneath their headpieces. And, so, to underline my mission, I set to memory one ode after another, and the sonnets and then to epic poems, stunning meek Sister Immaculata, making her swoon with my intensity and (I imag-ined) making Boron sear with my intrangisence.

If I am good at something, it is pitting one against another, as I did with my own parents — lying to one about what the other had said, taking sides in their arguments only to intensify them, stealing money then swearing I didn't — until that night my father, sitting in his chair, dropped his glass of Scotch and we saw too that he had loosened his grip on that gnarled limb of life that had been his. I felt mildly guilty, the way I had spent all those years brewing them toward discord, for no reason I can think of but my own entertainment. Sister Immaculata had no idea how I used her to get to Boron. Even as I knew it and did it, I felt a self-loathing. For some reason, I wanted Sister Immaculata to think I had seen some light, some revelation, when in fact I was swaddled in my own darkness, all through.

Memorization did not come easily to me. But I made the effort, just to see Immaculata's speechless stare. It is an acquired skill, I think. Once I had the hang of it I could retain almost anything. I learned to recite by writing the poems down and then throwing away the paper, which somehow made those lines unpurgable in my mind. Much later, my faculties honed from the poetry, I ran numbers, all of it up top, my command of those endless columns a marvel to my peers.

In school, Sister Immaculata seemed to silently wonder why no one snickered at my recitations, for they surely would have with anyone else. But these classmates of mine had been there for the disturbing scenes with Sister Boron, too, and in me they saw a troubling lack of center.

But eventually, I think, Immaculata figured it out. Maybe it was the way I sat sullen and uncommunicative in those moments before class began, while all the others merrily chatted. Or maybe someone had whispered in her ear — my school years had been marked and indexed by occasional but intense spells of fistfighting and wanton rule-breaking. She seemed to take a quizzical interest in my fractious nature.

I remember one particular day of connection. Sister

Immaculata, holding her tattered "Keats' Poetical Works," stared full at me and read from "Endymion":

> *Brain-sick shepherd-prince,*
> *What promise hast thou faithful guarded since*
> *The day of sacrifice? Or, have new sorrows*
> *Come with constant grief upon thy morrows?*

She stopped reading then, and kept staring at me until I had to look away. Outside, somewhere far off, I could hear a dog barking. I think that the others didn't understand.

There was a day, finally, when Sister Boron just wouldn't let it go. There was this matter of colloidal solutions. I could not produce an answer to her satisfaction, in fact I refused to say anything at all on the subject, just as I always had.

"Culhane," she said. "I asked you, What is a colloidal solution?"

I made a disgusted sigh.

"Culhane," she said, with a sense of summary. "You will not be humored. This is a basic question."

I said nothing.

"Your antics are through," she said. "This nonsense is over."

I rolled my eyes.

"You mustn't think you've won this," she said.

Now I had an audience. And that need to respond. I turned to my friend Fitz, who sat behind me, and whispered, "And who's keeping score?"

Sister Boron's keys hit me right on the crown of the head, the very eye of my flat swirl of hair, and the intertia was great enough that the keys deflected off my head and hit the blackboard, putting a crack up its length. For a stunned moment I watched the blood dripping on my gouged desktop without fully comprehending its source. Boron had a good arm. The droplets collected before my gaze, and I sensed them forming and dripping at my chin.

"Get out," she said, showing no sign of regret. I could not look at her. I got to my feet.

The day of the keys, I walked from that high school with blood starring my short-shorn head like a cleric's tight cap of devotion, and I forgot religion but could not shake from me those damned poems. I never saw Immaculata again, and wondered what parting words she would have had for me, had things worked out differently. As I lie here in a strange place in the gathering dark, I think of one, I believe it was John Donne, who said, if I am quoting at all correctly in this fog of recollection,

> *I am two fools, I know,*
> *for loving, and saying so,*
> *In whining poetry;*

How do I remember this, now? What use are these? Words to possibly live by? I don't know. I will say that Sister Boron did not easily fall away from the nexus of my hatred. In times of weakness, I thought of Sister Immaculata there without me, trying hard to go on with who was left.

From those school years I remember a line. I believe it was Aquinas: He said that man takes pleasure in the beauty of sensible things. But not I. Life went on. I scammed and cheated and fought my way into some self-sufficiency, if barely. I was a numbers writer for the Flaherty people, selling bets in the bars and corners I knew. I was paid a percentage and found a way of pocketing some of the looser cash, even though I knew I could get in unimaginable trouble, cut off fingers and so on. But my pick-up man was a cab driver named Shaughnessy, and I cut him in enough that he helped cover me. He was a crazy bastard himself, not to be trusted, and in our dealings Shaughnessy and I circled each other like sniffing dogs.

Getting collared was a constant worry in that kind of work. Most of the numbers writers tabbed bets on gas-soaked slips, and the guys down in Chinatown used rice paper they could chew down, and I heard a few guys even put the bets on smooth metal strips they could swallow and shit out again later. But no one ever challenged my retention of those long rows. My memory became legendary, in my own circles, and while some of my peers even had trouble getting every bet down, I could go a year with out one of my bettors challenging me on an overlook.

I had no skills and no other disciplines. Writing the numbers kept me moving forward. I found ways of rationalizing my increasing habit of skimming off the top. I tended to wheedle bets from nervous types, the ones I knew wouldn't have the guts to chase thrown-away money, and then I'd never record the bet. They were the types who were so far outside of things they needed me to tell them if they had won. These don't go as overlooks, I told myself. I figured they were too scared to start any trouble. I was 99 percent correct on that.

But one of my marks was overextending himself, and when his bets didn't pan out he started looking for loans. That led him to people in my organization, people I tended to avoid myself, and somehow an informational connection was made.

I lived with my mother, still, and that morning she answered the door and then came back to me, where I was still lounging in bed, and said, "Eddie, some of your friends are here to see you…"

That cloyingly suspect word — "friends" — made me sit up. I slipped out of bed and began to put on my clothes and told her to have them wait out front. When I had my shoes on, I went through the kitchen and out the back entryway. She followed. As I tried to close that door without a noise, I could see through to my mother's puzzled face.

"Eddie," she whispered. "Where are you going? I'm hard-boiling eggs for you..." And then I shut the door on her. I knew going out that they might even rough her up, just to send me a message, and for that instant I simply did not care.

But as I emerged from the back way I already knew these guys were too smart for that, and I hadn't even hit the bottom step before the big one reached out and had me tight on the arm.

"Eddie," the big one said. "Frankie wants to see you..."

"I'm in a hurry somewhere else," I said, pulling from his grip like a recalcitrant child. "I'll go see Frankie as soon as I can."

"We wouldn't be here if Frankie wanted to wait," said the smaller one, who was still bigger than I was.

"Let go of me," I said.

The big one shot the smaller one a look.

"Really," I said, dropping limp so that my knees were on the ground. "Let go of me..."

They started to drag me bodily, and I knew I was as dead as you could be, dead in one of a hundred heinous ways, and my bladder began to empty at the thought of the kind of gutting I was in for. Pissing my pants! People think they're tough and then these moments inform them. I felt that wetness and the pavement raking my knees and fingers digging into my flesh: and right then, then, I felt hot liquid spattering me from above, incongruous in its sudden arrival and combination with my own. I flashed back to Boron's keys hitting my head; in reality I was hardly touched at all on this: My mother, hanging out that kitchen window, had just dumped the whole kettle of boiling water out on my "friends." A hard-boiled egg glanced off my shoulder and squashed on the pavement before me, as if to aid my rumination.

It was the bigger guy who took most of the scalding, and his scream was cleansing in its sincerity. Now that's pain, I remarked to myself, even as I lay prone on the pavement. I flashed now from flashbacks of Boron to a scrap of a line of Keats — Now comes the pain of truth to whom 'tis pain — even as I struggled up and began scaling that rusting chain-link fence on my way towards escape.

It was right along this time where I began to see I was blessed with an uncanny luck, a cloak of fortune that underlined the rightness of my endeavors. After that long-ago day that Sister Boron's keys had bloodied my crown, very little had seemed to be able to touch me. After escaping Francis Xavier Flaherty's beckon, I hid, and slummed around, and avoided my mother completely, and never seemed to be found despite remaining in the midst of it all. My number-running was done, for sure. I was now on the outs with even that clan of true outsiders. But I wafted above it. I could not be touched. Things began to happen that made people notice me.

I got by brokering deals. I'd arrange for a truck to be stolen and then be driven into the side of a house, allowing the owners of each to make insurance claims. There were staged housebreaks, real housebreaks, and some that were sort of between the two. I burned down a few buildings, and those jobs paid well, but that made me nervous. I never carried a weapon, because somehow I had come to the conclusion that a weapon would scotch my luck.

There was my confirming moment, on a February afternoon when I was twenty-seven. I got cornered down in the North End, carrying a bag with stacks of cut paper banded to look like piles of cash, with twenties on the outsides. The deal in which this bag figured (as well as an amount of supposedly pure cocaine which probably was no more real than my cash) had gone very badly. We quickly became disenchanted with one another. A knife was produced for my inspection, and then I was running. Wild with self-preservation, breathless, I made my way up a highway ramp where the Expressway vaults over lower parts of the city. I was running along the narrow curb, my pursuer showing suprising persistence, and it was in that swirl of a moment that I faltered. What was I doing? It was that pain of truth: I felt abruptly and thoroughly informed of my bottomless failures as a man; before that knife could be shivved between my ribs I resolved that death was truly best when self-initiated. I stopped running and clambered up onto the guardrail, my balance becoming instinctual; my pursuer vacillated and fell to a tentative walk as cars on the Expressway began to slow.

"You're a sick bastard, Culhane," he shouted, sheathing his knife, retreating. "You're a chickenshit sicko bastard."

The implied end of my life had become a broader spectacle. Inside of five minutes there was a crowd, there were cops and news photographers, and yellow crime-scene tape being strung around me like a gay Saturnian ring. Below me, a Fire Department ladder truck grumbled up and telescoped its steps toward me as if in a handshake. And on the top of those scaling rungs, rising from below, grinning so demonically that I thought his gums would begin to bleed, was Jake McCord, former classmate at Holy Redeemer and now firefighter.

"I thought it was you, you green sack of shit," Jake said as the ladder met me, and he reached out to grasp my hand. Far below, the crowd began to applaud.

"Take my hand, scumbag," Jake said. "Take my fucking hand so I get a medal." Hunched on the rail like a monkey, I briefly pondered his certitude: son of a fireman who was the son of a fireman. Civil service, the wife, the kids and all else that my mother had wanted for me. No woman had ever deigned to touch me! No child carried my name! How had life made such a straight line for him, so that there seemed no need to ponder, so that existence seemed, as in the world of Sister Boron, to be informed by immutable laws and outcomes? I suddenly began to weep, for what I had become, and for what my mother had wanted.

"Look at the bleedin' poxy bastard, cryin'," Jake said, and he was nearly giggling in scorn. Only I could hear him, and it all must have looked different from farther away. I had the sense of telephoto lenses framing me tightly. I couldn't remember exactly what it was I had ever done to Jake.

"Shut up," I said, wiping my cheek.

"Fuckin' loser," Jake said. "Take my hand right now, you floatin' piece of crap."

"Careful, you," I said. His words smacked of all those schoolyard provocations, the ones I found so seductive and unable to recuse myself from.

"Like you'd really jump," he said. I could see down beneath us, a dozen of his fellow-men had their catch ring out, and were shuffling it under us. That circle of canvas was probably ten feet across, but from up on that rail it looked like a dime. I wondered if Jake was angling to throw me down at them. I wondered if such a tactic was safe. I thought, he wants to be a hero.

Mistrust, I believe, is a necessary evil. It would have made no sense to think Jake wouldn't try something. As I tentatively reached out, and his grin spread beyond all proportion, I suddenly, impulsively yanked him toward me. I'm not saying I was trying to make him fall: I don't think I'll ever know. Let us just say I prompted some redistribution of weight, and consequently of balance, and as Jake began to unbind from that ladder I felt his rough fireman hand clamping viselike on my more tender gambler's flesh, and I was no monkey after all, my sneakers sliding easily from that cylindrical rail.

We were a marvel of centrifugal force, falling, Jake and I,

bolos on a cord, in orbit of one another. The drop must have been forty feet but the attenuation of that moment makes the memory seem like some epic journey. Jake was shouting out as we fell, and in a terrified instant I understood he was in a delirium, punched out past fright.

And, in my own terror, I had forgotten about those groundset firemen, studding the edge of that catch ring, right until the moment I hit it. The softness of the impact came upon me like a missed note in a familiar tune. As their arms gave, I heard several of them groan. As one side of the circle collapsed from the force, I rolled off onto the pavement, stumbling over fallen firefighters, and I was on my feet and running. Running! In the shock of things, no one tried to stop me. No one was sure if I was a criminal, or what. I looked over my shoulder and they were all standing there, watching me spirit myself away. They looked hurt by my decampment.

And Jake: I read in an item in the newspaper that he had gone through a fiberglass topper of a parked pickup, gaining some cushion and, by surprise, living. My name was mentioned in the article. A fire lieutenant called me "the luckiest bastard who ever lived," and vowed that they'd find me.

My escapes had a rightness to them that barked, Destiny! How could these things just be happenstance? Against Sister Boron's rigid law-ridden physical world, with its blank progressions and reactions, came the ether of luck, unshakable, poetic, leading me like a stream back to its source.

But yet, at times, I had fears.

How I remember Sister Immaculata's rapture over my staccato recitations — I have a specific memory of how I took my class through Browning's "A Rhapsody of Life's Progress," in which the poet writes,

We lie in dark, swathed doubly around,
With our sensual relations and social conventions,
Yet are 'ware of a sight, yet are 'ware of a sound
Beyond Hearing and Seeing –
Are aware that Hades rolls deep on all sides
With its infinite tides

But even at the moment I mouthed those words, I couldn't get with the program, as much as I might have wished I could. The words hung on my skin like leeches, but couldn't work their way underneath and change my fundamental opposition to what they implied. I understood those passages, but couldn't feel them. Bad behavior and the invisibility of consequences can become so systemic that you gaze over at the good lives as if at a distant shore. I spoke the words, but I would kick the ass of anyone who dared simper at my quotations, or question my sincerity.

I can't remember anymore whose idea it was to do the bank. I do remember the moment right after that, when Fitz and I caught ourselves and had that mutual Ohhh of thinking, This is it, We have arrived. The plan was one in which there would be no shooting, that was definite, all the potential for gunfire neutralized by the swirl of the crowd.

There was this bank in Cod Square. We had noted that the armored cars had no option but to park on the crowded street, and that the crush of people particular to the Square at lunchtime was like a happy insulation. The money would be beyond the numbers, beyond the scams. We could go to a used-car lot and pay in cash. We could fill an entire shopping cart with the best liquor money could buy, with this job.

"What could go wrong?" Fitz said. "At worst, we can't do the job and we disappear into the crowd. At worst, we have to get out of town for a few weeks until things die down."

"Exactly," I said.

"We'll have the guns," Fitz said. "They won't have the guns."

"They won't have the guns?" I said.

"Not there they won't have guns," Fitz said. "Or if they have guns they won't use them."

"Then why do we need guns?"

Fitz looked at me. "How do you do a bank without a gun?"

"Fake guns," I said. "Or something."

"It's hard to get a good fake gun," Fitz said. "It's easier to just use a real one."

"Somebody could get shot up," I said. "I'm not into that."

"Then don't be in the deal," Fitz said.

"But it's my deal," I said.

"But you have to do it right," he said. "We're going to the next level. You have to do that right ."

So the plan formed, despite my reservations. All of a sudden, Fitz brought in my old partner Shaughnessy, with whom I had grudgingly done the numbers, and now Shaughnessy seemed even meaner and more desperate: His cab-driving days had ended with a floor of rolling empties and a completely unexpected telephone pole; when Fitz brought him in Shaughnessy went on and on about how strapped he was. I just kept staring at Fitz, like, What? This was a problem: Guys too desperate to score don't know when to quit.

Later on, I pulled Fitz aside at the Tap and I said, "Why do we need Shaughnessy?"

"He just kind of fell into it," Fitz said. "He sort of talked his way in."

"He's not trustworthy," I said.

"Not a one of us is," Fitz said. "Truthfully."

"Don't defend him," I said. Fitz just shrugged.

Later that afternoon, I saw Shaughnessy on the street, smoking a butt and looking into somebody's window across the way.

"Fitz says we never should have gotten you in this job," I said, not even sure what I was doing.

"Well I'm in, and I ain't gettin' out," Shaughnessy said without looking away from the window. "Fitz can kiss my arse."

Before I really had much time to think about it, there we were, sitting in a coffee shop watching the armored car work its way up the Avenue through the stalling traffic. You think of those things as taking months to plan out, but this was something like a week and a half after Fitz and I had sprung the idea.

Fitz had a gun. Shaughnessy had one. But I didn't. I had showed up that morning saying someone had broken the promise of a loaned piece, but the fact was I hadn't even asked around for one. My thought was to lay back and let the other two wave the weapons around. I would jump in where needed. I had promised them I would feign a weapon by keeping my hands in my jacket pocket, until they needed to be free for carrying bags of money. I knew I'd be flush by nightfall, and it wasn't going to go wrong and then I began thinking about having a little fun.

"Whoever's best with a gun should make the first move," I said, looking into my coffee cup. Fitz and Shaughnessy glanced at each other warily. No one took credit for being the best shot, although it was clear each thought he was; there was no discussion of when the best time was to show the weapon. But I knew what each of them was thinking, because I'd known them too long. Why did I love to put people against one another like this? All I knew was that there was a part of me that was enjoying it, forcing one of them to need to draw quicker; all I knew was that I'd be laying way back, and that without a gun I could just as well be a guy in the crowd. I could already feel the poison of betrayal seeping into every crevice of our flawed plan.

If things went smoothly, if we got the money before too many seconds went down, we would escape through the crowd, dump the bags in some bushes at a house two blocks from the Square, and then circle around with a stashed car and pick it up. This depended on our escape route, which snaked through several alleys and back yards and was guaranteed, Fitz said, to shake off any pursuers. It all seemed to make sense.

In that coffee shop, we were on three stools at the window counter, and Fitz put his paper cup in front of his mouth and said, "When the truck gets through that intersection we go outside." My stomach was tight. I realized I hadn't touched my doughnut. The bile of unease suddenly welled up within me, but it might have been excitement.

"Right now," Fitz said, and we were up and out on the street, snaking through the crowd, and we could see those guards coming out of the truck, jangling through keys, not really paying attention. This wasn't a million-dollar drop, just daily cash, but to us it was enough to make a play for.

From my experiences I can tell you that when things go desperately wrong it's like you can see retroactively the hundred little signals you had chosen to ignore. Fitz had the gun out way before he should have. Shaughnessy looked at Fitz and said, "You've got to be joking…"

Fitz stopped and screamed, "He said whoever's the best fuckin' shot…." We were still thirty feet from them but now any surprise to it was gone, and when I saw the nearest guard go for his holster I knew right then there'd be no money and the pooch had been desperately screwed and I needed to get out of there. And I was running, abandoning the other two like I once had my own dear mother. There didn't seem to be any noise, only the onrush of openings among the people, but then I heard the gunfire behind me, three shots, four, brought and returned, brought and returned, the play of different calibers. People were screaming now and throwing themselves down, and some time after that, it registered that someone had shot at me, and indeed had hit his mark.

Getting shot was nothing like I would have expected. The immediacy of the past tense, the rising sense that Something Just Hit Me! There was no perception of impact; the burn was like a steeping venom; it had caught me up above the right buttock, a bad place, although I would never have thought that beforehand. My leg began to weaken. I felt myself doing a grotesque semi-walk, a half-Groucho, like I was stumbling down a staircase that didn't exist. It was a gut shot and my clothes went red. I didn't feel anything real anymore and I kept running.

And I have made it another two blocks from there, and now I am in the soft soil underneath the porch of a house, where I have pushed through the crumbling lattice and then kicked it back into place, and I have been listening to the excitement of the people who live here as they stomp up and down those steps, trying to find out what happened, what the shooting was about, excited by their proximity to the event but not knowing how close they truly are. Light seeps in through the cracks of the floorboards above me. But the sense is only of night, of the dissipation of the moment.

One stuck memory of my long-dead father was of him putting rat poison under the cabinets, and telling me how the rats, after eating, would become intensely sick, crawling back into their holes to die. And here I lie, under a porch, bleeding into the soft soil, my indentation making a lazy S.

I am, after all, in the place all my actions have led me, choked of my own appetites. The truth of it is as clear as Sister Boron's admonitions, although for so long it never seemed that way, seemed that it just could not be. I could have seen that in the poetry, too, if I'd wanted to, but I suppose we use it as it suits us.

I am waiting for the dogs if they have them, dogs bellowing after the steam of my blood, and I am feeling light and ethereal and somehow my mind wanders relentlessly back to Keats, the doomed lover of Beauty, as he gathered himself for the finality, the inevitable decay of the corporeal. And, for no audience but myself, and for no purpose but to declare where it is I am, I dryly recite...

> *Save me from curious conscience, that still lords*
> *Its strength for darkness, burrowing like a mole;*
> *Turn the key deftly in the oiled wards,*
> *and seal the hushed casket of my soul*

A VISIT TO MY UNCLE

When I was seventeen, I went to New York City to meet my uncle, whom I had never met before. He was my father's brother, older by ten years. That trip, by dawn train from South Station in Boston on a mild March day in 1949, had come at my uncle's invitation, and though I went with the idea of asking him to do me a significant favor, I also had the feeling of an emissary, traveling with greetings to unknown places.

My father and my uncle weren't enemies, only strangers. They had grown up apart, for reasons beyond their control: Their mother had died, when my father was three.

What I knew of the story I knew from my father's side of it, bits and strings pulled together over years. Because my uncle, Charles, was older and about to go away to begin preparatory school, he stayed on at home, in the big family house overlooking the river where it turned and aimed itself for the Atlantic. James Shannon, my father's father, was an Irish immigrant businessman, specializing in linen and other imported fabrics. He had married an American girl, Alice Johnston: They had their first boy, she endured four miscarriages, then had a second boy. Then she died. My father, Paul, was too young to live with his father and brother. He was sent off to a more modest section of the same town, where he was raised by his mother's two sisters, maiden aunts.

Within this arrangement there surely must have been the tension of two sides reeling from a young woman's death. It would later be said that James Shannon had insisted on another child despite the obvious dangers, but no one will ever really know. My father and his brother were divided, I suspect, as if they were community property. The cracked and yellowing photographs I have of Dad as a child show a skinny boy in curls and a sailor suit, this at an age too advanced for such effects to seem darling. The aunts always did their best, my father said, but it seemed too that they had taken him on as a salvage project, to coax from his small being the last flicker of his mother. They commented frequently that he was his mother's very image. They taught him manners, daintiness of purpose, and infinite gentility. He loved the aunts dearly. This only heightened the confusion and vague sense of betrayal he felt when he entered school and got his first pasting.

The picture I have described may have been taken on the very morning he marched off to meet his destiny. I can imagine the aunts, one with her eye to the viewfinder of some primitive box camera, the other behind, fretting, telling him to smile. When he arrived home bloodied, the aunts wept while they dressed his wounds. They cried at the injustice of it all. My father also remembers how on the subject of alleviating this situation, they were notably mute.

But after the third beating, they quietly took him to the Little Gentlemen's section of Saunders Department Store and said, "Whatever you want, Paul." On this he was sketchy at best, having only been in school a week, having been so stricken with fear so quickly that he had enjoyed only limited opportunity to observe his peers. Yet he needed to decide. So he focused his mind on the image of the boy who had been beating him, a fourth-grader named Mulherin, and he chose clothes that, if not the image of Mulherin's, then were squarely in the spirit. Mulherin's rage at my father's ruffles indicated a passionate attention to matters sartorial. Indeed, in later photographs, he looks as if he's stepped off the "Our Gang" set, with his argyle sweater-vest, his knickerbockers and his high-topped shoes. And yes, he appears in these pictures to be a happy boy.

While my father spent his youth with the aunts, his father paid visits that came weekly, then monthly, then not much at all. James Shannon traveled in his business, riding Cunard liners back and forth to Britain, and when he went he was away for a long time. He could not have made an attentive father, but he was apparently generous enough in his financial support. Young Paul had clothes when he needed them and food and money for small diversions. When Paul made his way across town and passed the big house overlooking the river, it was almost always dark and silent.

When the boys were divided, Charles, barely a teenager, went off to a military school called The Forge. Charles came home on vacations and holidays and stayed with his father, and when James Shannon traveled, Charles traveled with him. Even though he didn't have to, Charles always wore his gray cadet's uniform. It was as if he had never gotten around to accumulating other clothing. And when he was home, he attended his own father dutifully, like a palace guard. On these occasions Paul was sent by taxicab to the front of the big house; most times, it was Charles who would be sitting on the front steps waiting for him. They would walk into the house together and sit on an upholstered bench outside James Shannon's study, until such time that they were called in.

The old man was not unemotional. When they finally saw one another, there would be a moment of contact that seemed genuine. Sometimes James Shannon would touch Paul's hair, or slap his back, and it would be then that the old man would sit and say, "Tell me how you've been, Paul!" And in the five or ten minutes it took Paul to tell of his life, the uneventful life of a boy his age, his father would be listening.

Charles's respect and affection for their father were clear; he seemed, too, to want things for Paul. During one of their infrequent holiday visits, when the three of them went into Boston to dine, Charles spent time telling him about his own life. It was a life of marching and schedules and responsibility, it seemed. Charles was commander of his wing of cadets and he told stories of problems he had solved for other boys, and of how he was going to make the military his career one day.

"When you get older, Paul, would you like to come down to the Forge?" he finally asked. My father, in his "Our Gang" outfit, said yes, he wanted to very much.

It wouldn't happen. The aunts simultaneously burst into tears when he mentioned it. He was still very young and they were horrified at the thought. Then regaining their composure, they added that if this was what he wanted, that he could, that if he wanted to someday go to this Forge and be a little soldier, that he most certainly could. He spent a long time pondering: The aunts were more of a family to him than his father and brother had ever been; even if he went there, it would bring him no closer to Charles, who by then was already off at college. So when the time came, he stayed home. James Shannon was said to be outraged, was said to have accused the aunts of turning a boy against his own father. No one asked young Paul to join the conversation, and it was then that James Shannon's visits stopped altogether, as if there had been an abdication. Paul went to the public high school, which he thought was fine, and when he finished he went to work as a reporter for the local newspaper. By then, his father was dead, swept away in an influenza epidemic; by then, Charles had gone on to law school and then to New York. This in a time when Boston and New York were very far away, when the estrangement of families could become more complete. Charles must have felt that as his father pulled back on young Paul and the aunts, that it was incumbent upon him to do so as well. The estate left by James Shannon was surprisingly modest, and offset by debts no one had suspected.

My father, as best he could tell, never felt particularly deprived. But as I grew up, I did, at least a little. I got used to hearing, usually from the aunts, about my Uncle Charles in New York. The aunts were getting on then. They would come to our house and sit together on the love seat and look after my father's needs, usually in the form of verbal commands to my mother. My mother tolerated the aunts gracefully. The aunts told the story of Charles and his success merely to set opposing sides. My father didn't seem to mind. "Oh, it's not that bad," he'd say. "So what if Charles has done well for himself?" When he said this, I was young. As I got older and the aunts began to drift away, one and then the other to a nursing home, my father once said to me, "All that about Charles — I think they just felt like they were put in a position, and that they resented it." He'd heard the complaints so many times they must have lost any sense of importance to him.

But, I wondered, hadn't he ever wanted to be reunited with his own brother? I was an only child, and had the feeling he must have craved some connection. I knew they were both grown men and that Uncle Charles was in New York, but the idea of having my rich and successful uncle know me was a powerful one. During the war, Charles had been called up from reserve and had distinguished himself in some manner, although as best we could tell it had not been in combat. Nonetheless, he been discharged as a full colonel. My father wasn't inducted, with his eye problems that would become cataracts and blind him late in life.

When I was a teenager he still had most of his vision, though it was weakening rapidly. Sometimes, I'd meet him on my way home from school and I'd walk with him to the eye doctor's office. I didn't mind. During my father's increasingly frequent trips to the ophthalmologist, I'd sit quietly and look at the equipment in the office, and try to guess what each one was for, what secrets it could tease from the darkness through my father's dilated pupils.

The doctor was a member of the Rotary Club, as was Dad, who by then was an editor at the town paper. They'd chat amicably in the darkness. In the end, this and other doctors couldn't do a thing for my father's eyes, which degenerated pretty much the same as they would have if left untreated, but there was a kindness in their actions that I appreciated, and came to want to emulate.

I did well in school, but I was also interested in pool. I knew I was devoting too many hours at Jim Mooney's Billiards on Eighth Street. Coming home late, I knew my father would be waiting, wanting to talk. I now realize that even at that age, I offered the kind of male companionship he'd been deprived of as a boy. At night, when I came home altogether too late, at an hour when most teenaged boys would be trying to sneak through a window, I would come through the front door and find him sitting up, slowly reading under the close-in halo of a high-intensity lamp. He'd be wanting to talk.

On a night like that, one rainswept night in the late fall of 1948, I told him I had the idea of being a doctor. He nodded at this, and he asked me if they were handing out medical diplomas at Jim Mooney's now. He smiled, though, because I think he was proud, if only of my self-assurance. I said, "I won't be going down to Jim Mooney's much anymore." I told him that playing pool had given me a chance to think, and this is what I'd been thinking about.

"Tell me your plan," he said. "Tell me how you think we can do this."

What he meant was that we couldn't afford it, and I knew it. His tone of voice said to me that if I had farfetched ideas, I better come up with a way of making it happen.

"Dad," I said. "I thought that Uncle Charles could help."

"Mark..." my father said. "I can't do that."

"A loan," I said. "Why can't we ask him for a loan?"

"Because we can't pay him back," my father said.

"Why couldn't I? I mean not right away, but eventually."

My father didn't say anything, and I held back with what I really wanted to say: That Uncle Charles had been the recipient of the family money when he was my age, that my father had been cut out of it, that the near nonexistent inheritance the aunts had more than once referred to was at least in part because of the expense of Uncle Charles's schooling. My father must have seen what I was doing as nearly begging, but I saw it as beginning to put claims on my father's fair share. I was speaking to him about loans, but in my way of thinking, it was something I would not be asked to pay back.

"Let's not talk about it now," my father said. "I'm tired and if we're going to talk, we should talk at length."

I went to bed feeling that at least the options were still open. I really did want to go to college, and really did think I might someday try to be a doctor. But it also seemed to me that this was a marvelous opportunity for them to talk. They hadn't in twenty years. We heard things from time to time, word filtering back through the loose web of mutual friends they had from town, but there was so much more I didn't know. I wasn't even sure if I had cousins.

The morning after I told my father I wanted to be a doctor, he brought my mother to the breakfast table and he had me tell her. She asked my father where we could get the money, and they began to talk about options. My father mentioned a second loan on the house, and about selling our second car.

"My eyes are getting so bad," he said, "it's ridiculous to own two cars."

"I could get a job," my mother said. "If Mark's away at college, I'll have time for something."

But I argued against these. I said to my father that because his eyes were going, he didn't know what would happen with his job. He looked hurt by this, and I would never have said it in any other context, despite its unspoken obviousness to all of us. There was no place for a blind newspaperman. I told my mother that if she was going to work, it should be because of Dad, and where it all seemed to be heading.

"I want to go to college, and then medical school, and you can't really afford it at all." They both sat quietly, thinking about this, and I realized I had augured for them the way their lives would go, that their own son had read them a sentence of a more-difficult life that none of his doctors were going to change. When, as I sat there, I realized what I had said, I wanted to apologize, or cry, or run from the room. But I sat there, and I said, "That's why we need Uncle Charles."

"Charles?" my mother said. "What's he got to do with it?"

"Mark wants to ask him for a loan, and to take the responsibility to pay it back."

"That doesn't sound like a good idea to me," my mother said.

Through the next week we made our way around one another, polite but quieter, and at times I wished I hadn't even brought it up. Thoughts of Uncle Charles failed to recede. I'd lie on my bed thinking about what sort of house he lived in, and tried to conjure the kind of life he'd lived that my father had been cut out of. I thought about that big house. I knew where it was, but hadn't been by it in years. One day after school I took my mother's car and drove to it, although I hadn't said where I was going. It wasn't a house anymore. It had been converted into a rest home. A fire escape ran up its side, and the front porch sagged with the years. I looked at it for a while, then started the car and drove home.

When I told my father that he should be the one to call Uncle Charles, he had said, "I understand that." One night at dinner he turned to me and he said, "If you want me to call Charles, I will."

"I do," I said. "It's a loan, and I would pay it all back."

That night he called his brother. The phone number was listed.

I sat at the kitchen table, trying to act like I wasn't listening. My father let out a long breath, picked up the phone, and made the connections through to New York. As he spoke with the long-distance operator, he stayed standing. After a bit, he made a small start, and I knew someone had picked up.

"Charles? Is this Charles?" he said. "Yes, this is your brother Paul. Paul Shannon."

He paused, and I waited, and then my father laughed and said, "It's wonderful to be talking to you, too."

My father asked him about his family, then he listened. He mentioned my mother's name, then mine, and then he said, "Mark is the reason I'm calling." He said, "Mark is thinking about his future, and he needs help." There was some more from Charles, and my father said, "I haven't even told you what he needs."

My fathered listened some more. "I'm sure he would," he said.

Despite the seeming good feelings, the call ended quickly (it was 1949 and calling New York was no small matter). My father said, "You're going to New York to talk to your uncle."

And so it was arranged. My father called Charles from his office to discuss particulars. I would take the train to New York on the second Friday in March, would meet Uncle Charles at his office at three o'clock, would discuss the matter of "help," and then I would take the commuter train with him and stay overnight with his family. I would meet my cousins, Mary and Margaret. I would meet my Aunt Sylvia.

The night of the call to Charles, my father, after describing what had been said, turned to my mother and said, "What do you know about that?" Despite his worries that Charles hadn't fully understood what was being asked of him, he seemed surprised and pleased at Charles's willingness to help.

As I rode the train to New York, I thought more about the planned dinner than about the needed favor that had necessitated this journey. The train got into Penn Station around one-thirty, and with several hours before the planned meeting, I decided to look around a bit.

The day was warm for March and I was wearing my father's overcoat. I sat on a bench in a small streetside park, afraid if I moved too fast I'd break into a sweat, waiting for the appointed time to arrive. My suitcase, with only a clean shirt and change of underwear and socks, was almost weightless. I gave myself twenty minutes to walk the three blocks to the office, which was on Sixth Avenue, and then stood on the sidewalk in front of the building until one minute of three. I didn't know what kind of law he practiced.

The building was old and magnificent. The woman at the front desk helped me stow my suitcase and coat in the cloak-room, and when I told her I was meeting my uncle for the first time, she said, "We all think a lot of Mr. Shannon." I was pointed down the long hallway leading to his office, but half-way there I saw a woman coming toward me.

"Mark, welcome!" she said. For a second I thought it might be Aunt Sylvia. I didn't really know why I thought that, but before I could embarrass myself she said, "I'm Mr. Shannon's assistant, Francine."

I was seated by Francine and handed tea, and then I waited.

Around three-fifteen, he walked in. I was stunned. In all the thoughts I'd thought about this uncle and this meeting, it had not occurred to me to wonder what he looked like. I felt then as if I were looking at my own father, who had somehow raced me to New York, dabbed theater makeup to gray his hair, and then rushed out to meet me. His glasses were even in my father's style, with the only difference in the lenses, which were much less thick.

"Mark, this is a wonderful moment," he said. His voice boomed the way my father's didn't (but could have). It was a voice of lawyerly self-confidence. He shook my hand and I stood gaping. His mannerisms were like Dad's in microscopic ways, despite the separate childhoods. It was as if this were an alternate version of my life, the one in which we had the money.

"Sit, son," he said. We settled onto opposite ends of a big red-leather couch that was there. "I've been excited about meeting you. How is your father?"

I told him about my father's failing eyes, and about how little could be done. Uncle Charles lamented this. "I was luckier on that account," he said, "although I'm not perfect by any means." He fingered the edge of his glasses.

I sat with my hands folded in my lap, and he said, "Your father tells me you need some help for college," he said.

"That's right," I said. "I know it's a lot of money, but I want to go to a good school."

"I applaud your ambition," he said. "I applaud your decision to want to be a college man."

"Thank you, sir."

"Don't call me 'sir,'" he said, but he didn't say what I should call him. "Well," he said, "I'd be delighted to help you out, and I'm sure there are ways that I can."

"It would be a loan," I said.

"I know it would, and I have some thoughts on that," he said.

"I would pay back every cent," I said.

He smiled, and nodded, and leaned back.

"What I would like you to do is study the law," he said. "I'm sure you've got the brains to do that, and at the same time I will be guarding my investment. I can see to it, if you are in the field of law, that you are given opportunities. I don't have a son, and the way I see it, you will be in a position to someday play an important role in this firm."

If I hadn't gasped right then, I felt as if I had. I looked around that office, and thought of these people I had met. It was the most generous offer anyone had ever made me, and I didn't realize, as I realize these years later, that nothing would ever equal it. He was offering to set me up. He was offering to grease my way into money and prestige, although I had done nothing to earn this opportunity. Yet I was confused, and I was worried. He was going to put me through school, but not the way I wanted.

"Did my father tell you my plans?" I said.

His smile faded just a bit. "That you want me to help you through school. Am I right?"

"Yes, sir."

"And?"

"I want to eventually go into medical training."

"Medical?" He didn't just say the word — "medical" — he said it in a way that made me know I'd hit a nerve. He said it like I had just told him I wanted to go to shit-shoveling school.

"Yes, sir," I said, caught in it now. "It was just something I'd been thinking about."

"But I can't do that, Mark," he said. "My associations are in law. Law is a very respectable profession."

"I agree that it is, sir. But I have to be honest. I've never even thought about being a lawyer." I didn't even know what kind of law Uncle Charles practiced. What had interested me about his law firm was the furniture, and the secretaries, and the silver tea service sitting on his oak desk.

"You won't even consider law?" he said. "That seems short-sighted. I've always wished your father had gone into it. I've always wished I could have done that for him, but we were young then, and I didn't have the means. Mark, it pains me that he is what he is."

"What do you mean?"

"That he's working in a newspaper," he said. "He deserved better."

"Did you ever ask my father what he wanted?" I said.

"I couldn't," he said. "We were separated and kept separated by matters we couldn't influence. Had I more influence, he'd be here, with me."

"Doctors do a lot of good work," I said.

"I wouldn't know," he said. "I've never been to one."

"Ever?"

"Ever, Mark."

"You've never been sick?"

"Of course I've been sick. But I heal the way they did in the old country. I get sick, I sleep until I'm better." He laughed then, at this bit of wisdom.

"It's not as if doctors are totally useless," I ventured.

My Uncle Charles chuckled. "They have a saying, which is 'First, Do No Harm.' I guess that's to remind themselves. What are those wonderful doctors doing for your father's eyes?"

"Not much, I guess."

"Not much. I see."

"There are some things you can't do much about," I said.

"That's what they said about my mother," Uncles Charles said. "And I'm sure they were right. But Mark..." he chuckled again. "Mark, I just don't have much use for them, and I just feel…hesistant…to loan you money for that sort of thing. Mark, I can help you in my own profession. I can help you."

"Well, I guess it's something to think about," I said.

"Exactly!" he said, and he seemed relieved. "That's exactly what I'd suggest." He looked at his watch, and he said, "We'll leave early today. I have a couple of short meetings, and I'll have to ask for your patience in this. Francine will bring more tea if you need it."

"Thank you, Uncle Charles."

After he left, I sat thinking. A lawyer? I realized my father would require an explanation if I came home saying I'd decided to be a lawyer; he wouldn't oppose me, I didn't think, but he would wonder what was going on. It occurred to me that I could get Charles to pay for part of my schooling, then refuse to study law when that time came. What could he do? What did I owe him? After all, my father had been cut out of every deal he might have had, and even if he didn't care about this injustice, I did. If I refused to commit to my uncle, I would be no closer to the life I wanted than when I had boarded the train that morning. I was in the middle of it now, and didn't know what to do.

When he came back into the office, looking more serious, and trailed by an unsmiling Francine, he looked over in a way that said he might have forgotten I was here, that the matters he'd gone off to attend to had erased the conversation we'd just had. It was only the slightest disconnection — he smiled and came toward me in a way I expected he did with his clients, warm and subtly self-assured — but it as suddenly changed my mind.

"I don't think I could do what you've asked, sir," I said. "Be a lawyer, I mean."

He sat there, thinking. His smile faded. "Do you think you

should talk to your father?"

"Maybe," I said. "He said I should make my own decisions."

He shook his head, like I was just thick.

"I want to help you, very much," he said. "And your father."

"I appreciate that, sir."

"I can give you opportunities your father didn't have."

"I understand."

"Well, I don't understand!" He was still smiling, but it was an incredulous smile. "I'm laying this out in front of you, and you're not accepting it!"

"I know. I feel very badly, acting this way."

He sat in his chair behind that big desk. "I never really got to know your father, Mark. I probably suffered more than he did about our mother's death, just because of the age. I was just coming out of childhood. I wanted to be with him. It was something that was impossible. All I had left was my father, and Paul was not a subject I could broach with him. I wanted your father to be a part of it, but it had all become impossible to do. It broke my heart that he went into newspapers. What could he have been thinking, Mark?"

I sat there in the big leather chair across his desk from him. "He seems happy to me, Uncle Charles."

He shook his head. "This is the way it has seemed, so often. I can help you, but it's not the kind of help you're inclined to accept. What you want, I can't really help you with."

"But I'd pay you back," I said.

"That's not the point," he said. "The point is different. This offer I'm making, this offer is not one I make to any young man who walks through my front door. I make an offer that I can live with. I won't extend it to you again."

"I understand that, sir," I said.

"Then I suppose there's nothing more to say." He took off his glasses and rubbed his eyes. "I have a few more meetings, and then I'm done," he said. "Then you can come to my home."

It was at that moment I knew I wouldn't see Uncle Charles again. When he went to his meeting, I asked to use the men's room; I washed my face and my hands, combed my hair. Francine's desk was vacant, and in the lobby of the building I retrieved my suitcase from the cloakroom and put on Dad's overcoat. Out on the street, I got to a phone booth, and I made a collect call to my father, at the newspaper. He came on sounding alarmed, and I told him what had just happened.

"You shouldn't worry about it," he said. "Just come on home."

I took out my train schedule, and we agreed when I would arrive back at South Station.

Near midnight, he met me at the train. His pal from the newspaper, Jimmy Bernard, had driven him in, so on the way home I couldn't say what I wanted to say. When Jimmy dropped us off at the house, Mom was waiting, and the three of us again went to the front room to discuss my future. My father made me recount everything, slowly, and then he thought for a while.

"So you're saying that you told him your plan was to be a doctor."

"Yes."

"And that being a lawyer simply wasn't what you wanted."

"Exactly."

"And that's how you really feel."

"Yes."

"So you've lost nothing," he said. "Charles can't do anything for you under those terms. You saw New York City and now you're home. You had a visit with your uncle." Then he thought this over.

"It's my fault, Mark. I should have told him about your plans. I didn't realize that things would work that way. I'm sorry."

And that was the end of it. I would still go ahead and try to be a doctor, and as it would turn out, my shortcomings would overtake me. By the time the realization would strike me that it was not to be, and could never have been, I would have come to find the compromises that would allow me to be content.

Those weeks after my trip to New York, we didn't talk about it. But on one night, late, I returned from Jim Mooney's Billiards, where I had gone once again to think, and I found my father in his chair, with his book face-down in his lap. Even then, he had begun the manner of reading I would know later, with the magnifying glass passing slowly over the pages.

"I guess I didn't say I was sorry about what happened," I said. "Down in New York."

My father shrugged. "It's funny," he said. "I hadn't even talked to Charles for so many years, but I never exactly felt we had broken things off. I don't know why I feel as if it has been now, as if it's something that's come to an end. That's probably a good thing."

Then he asked me to take out the trash. I meant to ask him more, to ask him how I could make it up to him, but when I came in he'd gone up to bed. He was a man for whom nothing fundamental had changed, and I don't think he ever expected to hear from his brother again. Indeed, when the letter came years later saying that my uncle had died, there was no talk of going to the funeral.

Conspiracy Buffs

Lyle and Deborah haven't been to New York before. The convention of the East Coast Assassination Investigation Workshops has finally brought them, at Lyle's insistence. Deborah has found, even coming in from the airport, that New York is as she has heard: The rudeness and all. She looks out of the hotel van and sees a grungy man in another car, staring at her, unabashed. It makes her look away.

"How safe do you think we'll be?" Deborah says.

"Like I said before, we'll be fine," Lyle says. "As long as we stay in the hotel or close by, we'll be fine. We'll be among friends."

Lyle and Deborah are both forty-eight. They live in Denver now, where Lyle services photocopiers and Deborah is in insurance. They have no children, and for this reason they have had the luxury of spending a week here. Lyle had wanted to go "all out" for this, and Deborah doesn't mind: In the regional conventions they've been to, in Dallas three times, and also in Portland and Kansas City, she has always found plenty to do while Lyle attends his seminars. Last year, in Kansas City, while he sat through "The Warren Commission: Footnotes and False-hoods," she had shopped and gone sightseeing and had long, contemplative lunches by herself. At the end of that, when they had returned home, Lyle holed up in his basement file room every night after dinner, sure he was on to something. Lyle feels he has made a breakthrough, and this is why they have come to the Big One, in New York. Their dogs, matching Lhasa apsos named Zapruder and Mannlicher, are being boarded at the veterinarian's.

Checking in at the hotel, Lyle is recognized. When he says, "Reservation for Lyle Asay," a man, off to the rear of them, says, "Umbrella Man." In this age of specialization, the Umbrella Man happens to be Lyle's specialty.

"That man's talking to you, honey," Deborah says.

"What?"

"Him. He said 'Umbrella Man.'"

Lyle turns, and with a grin he introduces himself. The man's name is Otto Litwak. He too, will be attending tomorrow's ten-thirty conference, "The Umbrella Man: Grassy Knoll, Sunny Day — Signals and Codes?"

"I am something of an expert myself," Litwak says, "although not of your caliber. Word has come from the American interior about your work."

"I don't recall hearing your name," Lyle says.

"I stay in Trenton," Litwak says. "I don't travel much."

All the way up the elevator, Lyle is ecstatic. Deborah asks him if he wasn't rude, saying he'd never heard of the man, but Lyle says, "But I never have."

While he is not on the panel selected to the conference, Lyle has planned to seize the floor and present his findings, which he believes will prove that the Umbrella Man was the linchpin of the conspirator's plan. Floor-seizings are a part of the culture, and he's already circulated word he'll be doing it. He was worried that he might not be known in New York the way he's been in Kansas City or Portland, but now that fear is laid aside.

"People are expecting me!" Lyle says. He's got the tan suit

on, with the big cowboy hat, as if he were a Texas Ranger, or maybe a cattleman.

"This is the big moment!" he says. "This is where they bite the bullet!" Then he says what he always says when he's excited: "Jack, you son of a bitch!"

Lyle has been saving up and doing his research for two years, waiting to be here, and his excitement has been further churned by the rumors that Oliver Stone will show up to speak. Lyle and his friends believe that Stone will be making a sequel to "JFK," and word is that he will hire three technical advisors for hundreds of thousands of dollars each.

Deborah knows very little about Lyle's theories. She prefers to ignore them. She believes in a single shooter. Had he known this before they married, it would have been a sign of incompatibility she knew he couldn't stomach. So she has distanced herself from it. "Kennedy's dead and we can't change that," she says to Lyle when he asks her opinion on things. There is an atheism in these words that Lyle clearly finds disturbing, and therefore avoids. It's been years since he asked. For the most part, their marriage is good.

All the way from the house in Denver, Lyle has carried his heavy briefcase with him, and now he is unwilling to trust it to the bellhop. Deborah has decided that his next Christmas gift should be a new briefcase, and that she will find a way of having a handcuff attached. She knows Lyle well enough to know he'd love it: it would be a semi-serious gift, like the pink pillbox hat he got her a few years ago. He has a flair for showmanship and paranoia. In the airport coffee shop in Chicago, waiting to switch planes, he had held the briefcase between his ankles while they ate.

In their room, when the rest of the luggage has arrived, he snaps open the briefcase and stacks his piles of manila folders on the table. Deborah hangs up their clothes, showers, and changes. At five o'clock, she says, "Lyle? Dinner?"

He looks up from his papers, as if she has just burst in unexpectedly. "Gee, Deb," he says. "I don't know if I can, with my conference first thing in the morning." He is nervous, she can tell. She shrugs. "I'll go down alone," she says. "I need to get out of this room for a while."

On the elevator down to the lobby, she doesn't feel upset. It's typical. After the Umbrella Man conference Lyle will attend another four and a half days of meetings, but he will be more relaxed, having gotten past his own highlight.

At the third floor, a man steps on the elevator, and she sees it is Litwak.

"Ah, Mrs. Asay!" he says. He is an eightyish man with the bearing of a professor. "Off to dine, are we?"

"Lyle's reviewing his papers," she says. "He wants to be ready."

"I should think you know very much about the Umbrella Man yourself," Litwak says. "What is your favorite aspect of the case?"

"Nothing, really," Deborah says. "I really don't pay much attention."

Litwak laughs. "I'm sure you're being modest. I know that my own accomplishments could not have amounted to anything without the support of the late Mrs. Litwak. I remember how she'd listen to each of my new hypotheses, and then rip it to shreds. Back to the drawing board! But you must know the main points of his argument."

"I don't think so," she says. "Did your wife really do that?" It seems that she has only seen men at these conventions.

When they get off the elevator, Litwak nods and shuffles off toward the street. In the hotel dining room Deborah has a club sandwich and orders a glass of wine, then looks in the gift shop before returning to the room. Lyle is in the same bent-in position as when she left.

"I saw your friend Litwak on the elevator down," she says.

This gets Lyle's attention. "What did he say?"

"Nothing much. Just hello. He was asking for you."

"Yeah? What was he asking?"

"He was asking about your work."

Lyle stands now, his hand still on a stack of papers. He has the umbrella out, the one he brings to conferences, to demonstrate various postulates. He also has a toy gun, a plastic Luger, to demonstrate the way it could be slipped beneath the furled fabric. Lyle has told Deborah that he has learned the necessary theatrics of such endeavors.

"I've never heard of this guy," Lyle says, and he picks up the telephone, retrieves a slip of paper from his pants pocket, and dials. "Fritz Reis," he says. Fritz is another buff from Denver, a close ally. He's staying at a less-expensive hotel uptown.

"Fritz? Lyle. Tell me if you've ever heard the name Otto Litwak." He listens. "No, no. I mean, now. He's here. I never have, either. But he knows my work."

When he hangs up, Lyle drums the desk with his fingers. "Fritz says he's never heard of him. Greg is there, and he never heard of Litwak, either. No one has ever heard of him."

Lyle picks up the house phone. "Do you have a guest by the name of Litwak here?" Lyle says. After a moment, he says, "You don't? I see. Thank you." He looks at Deborah. "Jack, you son of a bitch," he says.

Lyle and Deborah have been married twenty-two years. At first Deborah didn't notice the obsession in Lyle. He was someone who seemed to take a general interest. He had bought a few books. He was in his mid-twenties and seemed to have better things to do. The reading he did, of the Warren Commission Report and Death of a President and all the newspaper stories, indicated to her something vaguely cerebral. He was working as a fabrication engineer then, and the after-work investigations seemed a break from the pressure.

The twentieth anniversary of the assassination, however, seemed to set him off. The company had been downsizing, and Lyle had taken a buyout and tried to start of his own company, selling public-domain software. He had a little office in their basement, and a lot of free time as he sat there waiting for people to phone in orders. It was then that he began to see the whole grand scheme.

It didn't start with the Umbrella Man. It started with the puffs of smoke from behind the wall. He began researching weapons and ammunition, trying to determine what might have caused the puffs of white. He tried to be a generalist. He tried to delve into Ferrie and Shaw. But as he studied photos taken across the Grassy Knoll, he couldn't get his mind off the Umbrella Man.

The first order of tomorrow's meeting will no doubt be the discrediting of one Louis Witt, who came forward in the Seventies to claim he was the Umbrella Man. He had explained himself by saying that the umbrella he opened on that sunny day was symbolic of appeasement, a reference to Chamberlain's rolling over for Hitler on the rainy day in Munich. But trashing Witt is always a prelude to the real talks, like an invocation. Lyle once got Witt on the phone, years ago, and with a tape recorder running and a suction-cup microphone on the receiver. He shouted at Witt until the man, after demanding to know how Lyle got his phone number, hung up. Deborah remembers the redness of Lyle's face after that call, his wild-eyed look; she remembers it because he has it now, thinking of Litwak. Deborah has put on her nightgown and gotten into bed. Over in the corner, Lyle is still going over his documents.

"Honey," she says, "come to bed. You need to rest."

But a little before six, when she awakens, Lyle is still at the table, in his clothes. Has he slept and then gotten up again? "Lyle, are you all right?"

"I'm fine," he says. "I'm ready." He stands up and his hands move toward his back, which stiffens when he does these all-night sessions. "I just need a shower," he says.

She knows he won't go down for breakfast, so while he's in the shower, she orders room service. He's still in the bathroom, shaving, when the food comes, scrambled eggs and toast and orange juice and coffee. In a hotel bathrobe, he eats quickly, without talking, and then he gets dressed, knotting a dark blue, square-patterned tie that matches exactly Kennedy's on that day: The Kansas City convention had a guy in a booth selling these ties and PT-109 tie clips, all of which sold out almost instantaneously.

"In case you need to know, I'm going to go to Macy's today," Deborah says. "Then Bergdorf Goodman." He hasn't asked, but she says, "I don't want you to worry."

Then, distracted, Lyle says, "Where's my umbrella?"

"I don't know," Deborah says.

"It was right here on the table. When I went in the shower."

"I never touched it, honey."

"I don't believe this," Lyle says.

He looks all around the room, then in the closet, under the bed, and in the bathroom. "It's gone," he says.

"It's got to be here somewhere," Deborah says.

"It's not, can't you see that?" he says. He stands, rubbing his bottom lip with his fingertips, and then he says, "Who brought the food?"

"Oh, Lyle, come on."

"Is there any other explanation?" he says. "Is there any other explanation?"

"I don't know," she says.

"Now I have to find a new umbrella!" he says. He goes to the table, takes his plastic Luger, and puts it in his waistband at the small of his back. He puts on his suitcoat, hefts his brief-case to his side, and then he's gone.

Within ten minutes, Deborah finds the umbrella, underneath the folded-back bedcovers. Yes, she realizes that the boy from room service had to move the umbrella from the table, so he could put the tray of food there. She finishes dressing, and on the way out, she takes the umbrella with her.

In the lobby of the hall where the convention is taking place, she finds the registration-and-information table. "I'm trying to give this to someone," she says, holding out the um-brella.

"We don't go for pranks," the man at the table says. He is wearing sunglasses and has a beige wire snaking from his col-lar up into his ear.

"No, honestly," she says. "My husband thought he had lost it, but it's found. He really may need it."

"Listen," the man says, "There are a hundred and ten people in that room, and I can count on one hand the number of people who walked in without an umbrella. If he needs to use one, he has plenty to choose from."

"No," she says. "He needs this one."

The man jumps to his feet. "Hey," he says, "we don't want any funny business here."

In Bergdorf Goodman, she decides she shouldn't have thrown Lyle's umbrella in that trash can, but she knows she'll never get it back. She had walked from the information table and out of the hotel lobby; on the street, she saw that the day was cool and brilliant, and had disgustedly relieved herself of the umbrella. Now, she knows she'll never hear the end of it if she doesn't admit it was stolen.

She likes crowded places, and moves through the store slowly, rustling against passing shoppers as they squeeze by islands of merchandise. She can't help but think what Lyle often asks when they are in a well-known place: "Can you imagine what it was like here on that day?" Lyle's memory of all that is sharply defined. He grew up in Delaware, and he recalls being on the broad lawn outside his high school gym, playing touch football, when he heard.

Deborah has told Lyle that she doesn't remember what she was doing when she heard, and that used to throw him into a rage until he came up with a restyled theory: She had been in shock. Actually, she had not been in shock, and remembers precisely what she was doing. She was on her first date with her hottest flame ever, Westy Dodd. They had only commenced their travels, and were sitting in a soda shop in her hometown of Bradford, Pennsylvania. Someone, some face from her high-school homeroom, ran into the place and said, to his friends in a near booth but loud enough for everyone to hear, "Somebody shot the President!" If she had a reaction, its intensity has faded in memory, and what she remembers is the brief thought that this date would be ruined. Then Westy — his slicked-down blond hair gleaming in the fall light — reached across and took her hands in his, and said, "Let's choose not to be unhappy." She remembers thinking, That's all right with me. By nightfall, as the nation mourned, she was making out with Westy in his father's Rambler. It only lasted a month, but by then, everyone had adjusted, and she had seemed to just float above the sadness.

Of course, everyone has their memories, and hers, she knows, only matters in light of Lyle's passions. But yet it is a memory that would have otherwise been lost, or filed away, or blunted.

After she finishes her shopping, she takes a cab back to the hotel. When she comes into their room, the person she sees is Fritz. He's a thin and graying man, probably about her age. He's sitting on the edge of the bed with a plastic hotel cup filled with ice and his usual Dewar's.

Greg is at the table, staring at the television. He is a fat kid of twenty-one or twenty-two, whom Deborah and Lyle met in Kansas City. He's come over to the assassination theorists from the Star Trek crowd, he says, because he has come to understand how the assassination is the root of almost everything important, including Star Trek, which he now understands was a massive homage to Kennedy and his vision.

"Hail to the Queen!" Fritz says, raising his cup. Greg, in a T-shirt that rides above his beltline, revealing pale and copious flesh, simply says, "Deborah."

"Your husband struck fear in the hearts of the Darts," Fritz says. The "Darts" are the Umbrella faction that espouse the theory that the umbrella on the grassy knoll was actually a clever weapon that shot tiny poisonous darts. Lyle's theory is that the umbrella, which is seen sideways in the photographs, was held high on the shaft as the Umbrella Man brought a pistol close to his eye, to achieve the accuracy in the shot that hit Kennedy's neck, the wound that was passed off by conspiracy-connected doctors as an exit wound. Lyle believes that should the real umbrella ever be found, it would have a small hole at its very edge, pre-cut to accommodate the gun's muzzle. The lack of that hole proves Louis Witt was not the Umbrella Man.

"Where's Lyle?" Deborah says.

"In the shower," Fritz says. "Then we're going to dinner."

"Oh," Deborah says.

Lyle is just coming out of the bathroom, wrapped in a towel, carrying his own drink. "I didn't think you'd mind, Deb," he says. "We have so much to review."

"I only made reservations for two," she says.

"Already changed them," Lyle says.

But they don't get in at the restaurant they've chosen, because Greg refuses to wear a tie, putatively on principle. They end up at a vaguely seedy diner a couple of blocks away. The place serves beer, and the men resume their drinking. Lyle is still glowing. He has not yet even mentioned the lost umbrella, to Deborah's relief. The three men fall into a rehash of the day's event.

"Can you believe them?" Lyle says of the Darts. "I mean, what's their problem?"

"They're crackpots," Fritz says.

"I mean, why not just make a big joke out of the whole thing?" Lyle says. "Why not just mock the man's legacy?"

Fritz turns to Deborah. "You should have seen your old man in there. He took the floor away from the panel. People were listening, and I could hear some of them whispering, 'Who is that?' Lyle just knocked them dead. His reconstruction of events was so — logical! They just sat stunned when he was finished."

"The Darts were met, and found wanting," Greg says.

But Lyle isn't talking much.

"Honey?" Deborah says. "Are you all right?"

Lyle allows a semi-grin. "I'm fine," he says.

"It's that Litwak that's got him worked up," Fritz says.

"That Litwak's an odd duck," Greg says.

"What did he do?" Deborah says.

"He was just there, hanging at the edges," Fritz says. "Very suspicious, you know? Very weird."

"Is he a Dart?"

"He's not anything," Greg says, in a nearly-annoyed way. "Don't you see the point? An unknown man appears, by coincidence, as Lyle Asay is checking in, coincidentally bumps into Mrs. Asay on the elevator, proceeds to grill her about what she knows, coincidentally appears at a convention as Mr. Asay reveals what may be the key to the entire conspiracy."

"He didn't grill me," Deborah says.

"They know that approach doesn't work," Fritz says. "They're very sophisticated."

"What are you trying to say?" Deborah says.

"He could be very dangerous," Greg says. Lyle nods gravely.

"Oh, come on," Deborah says.

"I'd replace that plastic Luger with the real thing," Fritz says.

"Most women just don't get these kinds of things," Greg says.

Deborah says nothing more, and the others quiet down and slowly sip from their beer glasses. There is a cursory parting on the street; walking back toward their hotel, Deborah says, "I mean, Lyle, My God!"

"They're my friends," he says. "They're looking out for me."

"Do you really think you're in some kind of danger?"

"Man checks in under an assumed name, comes literally out of nowhere," Lyle says.

"He came from somewhere," she says. "Everybody comes from somewhere. I think he mentioned Trenton."

"Yes," Lyle says. "But there is the one key fact, the indisputable thing: An umbrella, stolen from a hotel room on a cloudless day. Explain that one away."

They walk the rest of the way without speaking. In the hotel room, Lyle undresses and gets in bed. "I didn't sleep last night," he says, and then he is asleep. It's not even nine o'clock. She wants to put on the television, but she's afraid it will wake him. She takes the room key from his pants, takes the elevator to the lobby, and sits on a couch facing the front entrance. She is in New York and wants to watch the world go by.

After an hour or more has passed, she sees Litwak coming in. He is small and precise, dressed in neutral fastidiousness. He sees her and smiles, then approaches.

"Your husband was quite marvelous today," he says.

"He'll be happy to hear that," Deborah says. "I told him we'd spoken, and he wanted to invite you to join us for dinner. But you weren't registered here."

"I am with my friend Stein," he says. "We split the costs, so that Mrs. Stein won't think we're being frivolous." He turns and signals a man who has been hovering nearby. "Bill, come meet Mrs. Asay." Stein is also elderly. "We're both retired from the transit authority in Philadelphia," Litwak says. "We share this common interest and decided this convention would be quite a lot of fun."

"And has it been?" she says.

"Beyond our expectations," Stein says. "So many fascinating theories."

"You know, they all spy on each other," Deborah says. The two old men look at each other approvingly.

"I was formerly a numismatist," Stein says. "But that crowd has gotten unforgivably dull. Besides, looking at coins strains my eyes now. Otto brought me in from the cold."

"We are discussing our own umbrella theory," Stein says. "But of course we can't reveal it. Perhaps next year."

"I'm eager to hear it," Deborah says.

A while after the men have gone on the elevator, Deborah rises and makes her way up to the room. As she comes through the door, Lyle starts, staring from his side of the bed, but then his eyes roll back and he's asleep again. She realizes in these moments that they have both begun to age. Deborah knows that the vacation will get better, as they always do. By tomorrow he'll be more himself.

She thinks of Lyle as he was, as he must have been, a young man racing across a field, waiting for the football to descend into his hands, a boy only moments away from hearing the news. He will never shake the idea of a conspiracy, it informs his days; but in that moment of his youthful narcissism he will see that not as a crime against a man he never met, but against the very person Lyle was and could have been. Lyle, the young man going old, now rolls over to his side so that what she can hear is only the soft snore against the blankets. What pictures form in his head she cannot say.

Notes Toward My Absolution

Here is my contribution to a moral world: When I rob convenience stores, I have put no bullets in the gun.

I come in all business, but I lay the gun across my heart, like I'm saying the Pledge of Allegiance. The barrel points off at a benign angle. I've never aimed my gun directly at anyone, because I've never had to.

The first words I always say are these: "I'm completely calm."

Then I say, "We're not going to have any problem here, are we?" I negotiate. I look for cooperation.

Still, they're scared, and why not? On robbery nights, I cruise looking for the stores with the women, or the skinny teenaged boys, or the slow-moving semi-retirees. I avoid people who might try to be heroes. Women, they see by my tone of voice that I'm not out for rape or violence, and they seem to feel better. I can talk to people. My wife says that women find my voice trustworthy, and she says that's what first made her love me.

Running out of one of these stores with my canvas bag of money, I've tried to think of something to say. Even in a robbery, there are moments of social awkwardness, and I find mine at the completion of the act, when my victims seem to seek out validation. I used to think they wanted to be reassured. An aside: I once said to a woman, "Put all the cash in a bag," and she said, "Paper or plastic?" Then she realized, and she had to surrender a quivering smile, and I'm sure she could see the grin from the mouth hole of my ski mask. I said, "Paper," because that's another of my contributions to a better planet. But this laughing threw her off, I could tell.

One night, running, I yelled back, "I have no bullets!" I waited for a look of relief, but the face of that cashier, a gap-toothed girl with stringy red hair, it was pure hurt. Driving, I thought, Of course. Wouldn't she naturally feel duped? Wouldn't she somehow feel dumb? People would make fun of her, for being robbed by a man with no bullets. I don't want that. I think of these all-night convenience store clerks as friends. I feel paternal.

They'd never know. The ski mask covers my gray hair. When I get ready to go out to rob, my wife lets me use shoulder pads from one of her sweaters, the kind with Velcro so as to stay in place. I take on a blocky look, becoming a man of indeterminate age, race, orientation. At dawn, before breakfast, I jog on a golf course near my home, and I finish up with a vigorous set of wind sprints. When I turn and flee from the scene of the crime, I want a youthful springiness. I run for my car feeling boyish, frisky. Crime is making me young again.

I worked for years in the high-tech field. My wife and I, we raised three kids and put them through college. We sold our home, which sat in the foothills, and moved to our condominium near the golf course. I looked forward to early retirement, seven, eight years ahead. But then the company let me go.

Our friends assume that someone like myself — well-educated, a long-time employee — would have had an attractive severance package, a hefty pension. We let our friends think that, though the truth is much less civilized. But I've tried to remain of the conviction that there is no room for anger. To allay their worries, we entertain. They come to dinner, where we serve fine food on our plate-glass dining table, beneath our many-bulbed brass chandelier. We feel especially buoyant on these evenings, carving out sirloins paid for from the rifled cash drawer of an all-night store in the bad part of a town many miles away. After our guests leave, the instant the door is shut, my wife begins to giggle, and I bear-hug her, telling her to be quiet, that they might hear.

How did I first broach the subject with her? I told her straight out. I had the gun, and I was about to go, and I told her. I thought she'd try to talk me out of it; I had assumed that. She didn't. This was after many weeks at home, searching through the Help Wanteds. It was at a time when no companies would even consent to interviewing me. Bills were accumulating, and we felt the shame of my sitting long days at the kitchen table. She would stand at the edges of the scene, in the shadow of a doorway, looking at me.

There were brief times when I had considered suicide, but I wouldn't call that a serious option. I didn't want anybody getting hurt. But this was significant in that it was the first time in a long life that the thought ever crossed my mind. I would drive for hours, thinking about what it was I thought I would do. One evening, in the midst of this, I stopped at a 7-Eleven to buy stamps. The clerk was a cow-eyed girl. She was talking on the telephone, ignoring me. It's never been my style to raise my voice. I waited. I began to feel as if I suddenly radiated a thick musk of impotence. She talked and talked.

My professional field, the life I was forced to abdicate, is a young man's game, at least in the eyes of those who hire. At my outfit, which conducted research in supercomputers, there's always a new microkid. My education and experience count for little. I had some version of power, and then I was managed out. But I'm coming to tell myself that I don't mind. I remind myself of how I used to spend my days in grim solitude, staring at diagrams of microscopic circuits. My most common temporal reference was the nanosecond, even while great chunks of years slipped liquidly past. Now, my wife and I go to local restaurant for the Early Bird Special, where we chat over leisurely meals. We then go home. After a lengthy nap, I leave my wife in the living room, use the bathroom, then go to the car with my briefcase, which contains my ski mask, gun, shoulder pads and a foldable raincoat.

On the highway, looking for a distant store in a distant town, I feel that my new work has begun to let me see the world. My Lincoln Town Car is quite comfortable, and the mileage isn't bad, and I'll drive forty, fifty, sixty miles to do the job. I listen to Rimsky-Korsakov's Scheherezerade, Op. 35. I turn it up and feel my car barrel effortlessly forward.

The only person who can be hurt is me. No bullets! I haven't even the strength to pistol-whip. I am the only person in danger.

———

When I return, we sit at our table and count out the money. Fifty, sixty dollars, that's the average take. My wife always asks me to describe how it went.

"Tonight I visited a store in Lakewood," I said last time. "The girl there looked a bit like Andrew and Betty's daughter, what's her name?"

"Kathy?"

"Right. She looked like Kathy. When I came in, she said, 'Oh, my fucking word.'"

"The language!"

"It's terrible. But common. I said, 'No problem. Just the money.' I whisper now, you know. I don't want them hearing an old man's voice. I give them this rough whisper. She put the money in the bag, and I told her to lie down on the floor an count to one hundred."

"Good!" my wife said. "It's incentive for them to wash their floors once in a while. Do you ever look at the filthy floors in those kinds of places?"

"So I went outside, back around behind some of the other stores in the same shopping center, which were closed. The briefcase is there, open. In goes the gun, ski mask, raincoat, shoulder pads. I'm a gray-haired man in a nice suit again. I pause a moment to comb down my hair. I come around, make sure the police aren't near, and I go to my car, which is parked away from where the cashier could have seen it."

"What if the police had come and seen you? How would you explain being back there?"

"I'd tell them I saw someone running from the store. I'd say I was trying to see where he was headed. They'd thank me as they ran into the darkness."

We've seen no bulletins, no pattern recognition. Nothing appears on television or in the newspapers. No talk of a "crime spree" with its connotations of manic overindulgence. Convenience store robberies are written off in the bookkeeping, the way I was.

After a job, when the cash is in orderly piles, we look over the household budget. What are things we can afford? We've become light eaters, and we have closets full of clothes. Gas, electricity, water. Insurance premiums. Property taxes. Dues for the homeowners' association. But no mortgage now, thanks to the favorable sale of our home. We usually balance out our finances quite nicely, with this small bit of padding. Our children keep calling to offer us money. It's nice to be able to tell them no.

Tonight, I'm not sure where to go. I feel quite well, full of roast beef, dressed in my favorite autumn-weight worsted. I only regret that I must wear my gardening shoes, because they're the only ones that look right for a robbery. I wouldn't want to be betrayed by my favorite wingtips! My wife suggests the future acquisition of elevator shoes, or perhaps some of these fantastically ornate basketball shoes I see the kids wearing. When we're at the mall we look them over, comparing prices, waiting for clearance sales.

The sun, as I drive, is dipping down beneath the winter landscape. The sky is both cold and embracing. Where to go?

I drive toward the interstate, passing many possible places in which to do business. Liquor stores I stay away from, and Mom-and-Pop stores. These are small business owners, whose livelihood depends in part on fending off criminals. I go by them, guessing which ones would be armed. "Shotgun," I say aloud as I go by the beer-and-wine shop in which I can see a burly bearded man behind the counter, watching television.

These convenience store chains don't allow their employees to be armed, so the police are my only worry. But I'm an intelligent man, and I can handle that. I used to go to Neighborhood Watch meetings, complaining bitterly about the utter lack of manpower the police seem to have. Ha!

I drive on, and when I hit a bump or rise, my gun thumps inside my briefcase. Me, a gun! Who says people can't change and grow after midlife? Getting a gun is an incredibly easy thing. Many an older gentleman like myself keeps such a gun in a drawer in his night table. When I filled out the forms and picked my weapon, the man at the store eyed me skeptically, and I knew exactly why. We've read the stories, about said older gentleman mistakenly shooting his wife as the poor lady emerged from a nocturnal trip to the bathroom, his fear of helplessness having become honed to a dangerous edge. The shots, the blood. Then the realization that the warm lump next to him in the bed is nothing more than the many pillows we accumulate as we age.

For the gun, I paid by check, and gun-store man asked me how much ammo I needed. "I'm all set," I said.

How moral, one may ask, is this whole scenario? Could I not draw on personal savings to get me through to Social Security? Don't I believe I can ever find another job? Must I pick on those I admit I view as weak (although all of us are surely weak when standing before the barrel of a gun)?

These thoughts do weigh on me. The answer may well be that I need not resort to crime, but that I am swallowed up in the necessity to act.

My wife worries, as much as she thrills to all this.

"When you make your getaway, do you speed?" she says.

"Getaway?" I say. "Getaway? I sound like John Dillinger. Imagine, my humble Lincoln as a getaway car. You, dear, would then be my moll." We giggle again. Then she says, "But remember what happened to Dillinger. In a pool of blood outside the Biograph Theater. He never suspected it would happen then."

"When does it stop?" she said tonight. I told her I didn't honestly know.

"It will have to stop, somehow," she said.

"As soon as I find a new job," I say, although we both know I've just about given up trying.

After I lost my job we did much to laugh about. We stared at each other with far-off, vaguely disappointed looks on our faces, still in mild shock about how abruptly my career had come to an end. I had the sense that I had no more control over my life. For a professional man, control becomes an essential, if too easily accepted, way of life. My wife, she had done her part, and she deserved a comfortable, predictable future, and it has been ripped away from her.

It happened like this: The plant manager, a fellow named George, called me into his office. Most of us worked in cubicles, but George had a glass-walled office with stainless-steel furniture. I sat, and George told me to hold on, and called in Bernie, the product manager, my direct supervisor. I thought they had an important project for me.

When the three of us were seated, George said, "Bernie has to talk to you." He said. "I have to go to the bathroom." We both watched him exit, and then Bernie, looking more trapped and angry than I, said, "Hey, Gene, what can I say? It's business."

And this is business, too: When I rob stores, these nodes of a vast corporation, the loss is factored in. My arrival is expected, to confirm the numbers. The cashier still goes home with minimum wage. My contribution is that I cycle this money back into the economy. And the cost goes directly back to ourselves, the consumers. Although I deal with the cashiers, it's not them I mean to hurt, to terrorize. It is a moral decision, then, to create for them discomfort but to really, truly, have more lofty aims.

I'm sitting in the parking lot of a shopping center, in which a Store 24 stands glowing, waiting. It's well after midnight, and I should call my wife. This trip has taken me over the state line, into the thrill of new jurisdictions. I am off behind another car, at a severe angle, and I watch the coming and going of people, lazily making their small purchases. There's no hurry. I'll wait until that sudden settled moment when I know it's time. The gun is next to me, as harmless as a grapefruit.

And as I wait, I sit in my car, running the heater, a hundred and fifty miles from my home, my heart beginning to throb. I'm about to go in, and see absolutely no reason that there'll be a problem. I'll come bounding out, and in my plushly appointed car I'll jump onto the interstate. And some time later, miles away, I am likely to find myself quivering as a state trooper comes floating up behind me, exerting an urgent pressure. I will, as I have before, feel the depressurization that is always a part of being found out. And then, behind me, no lights will go on, no siren will sound. The trooper will become annoyed by my leisurely pace, and will linger at my bumper before passing, vanishing up the road, engrossed in his own concerns, dismissing me again.

Travels With Mr. Slush

My first confession: I'm not *the* Mr. Slush. It's just that when I'm in that truck, I take on the persona. You get behind the wheel of that vehicle, you hit that toggle switch that activates the tinkle-tinkle-Pop-Goes-The-Weasel 250-watt-per sound system, and you're Mr. Slush, the one and only.

The route they gave me is in the South End. You really have to work for a sale there. But I don't have much of a choice. My probation agreement said I had to have a steady job. My lawyer's brother-in-law had the Mr. Slush franchise for this part of the state; Armand, my lawyer, told me that to get the job for me, he was getting out on a limb. So don't screw up, he said. I could only stand there saying Right, Thanks.

There was no training to speak of. Before he sent me out on my first run, my boss, Arthur, told me The Two Rules:

Rule One, no freebies.

Rule Two, watch out for kids running at your truck from behind parked cars.

Rule Number Two is the hardest to follow. I troll the streets, "Pop Goes the Weasel" at full volume, looking for action, and when there's none, I have to fight the urge to crush my foot into the gas pedal. I work on commission, and I have to find the good places, the rich veins of children and coin. You go and go, and then all of a sudden some kids are darting out in front of your wheels, waving. Or you look in the rear-view and there's a pack of them on bicycles, running you down. I've added Rule Number Three: Don't stop too quickly when kids on bikes are after you. I'm lucky that one didn't get hurt, except for the cuts. Most times, they're on you without warning. Drying out, I used to have dreams of animals grabbing me by the flesh and tearing me to pieces, and I sometimes flash back to that as the kids come at me, screaming and pushing. Totally gluttonous. At the public pool, where I pull up on the grass, so many of them descend upon me that when I'm done, I have to do a visual of the bottom of the truck, to make sure nobody's gotten underneath to curl sleeping in its shade. The little ones, they trust Mr. Slush too much. My boss, Arthur, isn't sure he trusts me at all. He knows the whole story, because Armand sent him the case files. Theft, deceit, self-destruction — it's all there. The day I met him, he said that if I was willing to pull myself together and get with the program, that Mr. Slush could be my ticket to the good life.

"Learn the ropes, maybe get a franchise yourself somewhere," Arthur says many mornings, while we load ice blocks into the crusher. "Having your own business builds self-respect like nothing else."

He has four trucks, and in the mornings we all work together, loading up with the ice and the mix. The others are college kids, mostly. I'm not a whole lot older than them, but different, of course. We'll spend the summer working our routes, and then when they go back to school, I'll stay on. I'll cover the city my-self until the weather goes cold in late fall. Mr. Slush is a sea-sonal being. In the winter, Arthur drives one rig down to South Carolina, where he spends the darker months doling slush to retirees on the broad beaches. He says that if I prove myself, he may let me take a second truck to an adjoining community.

Arthur mixes the lemon syrup, still talking about my future. He imagines me not only clean and sober, but stuffed with self-worth: "I wait at five o'clock for you guys to come on home," he says, "and when the trucks pull in, one after another, I feel like I've made something of myself. I feel like I have carved out my little place in the world." He looks at me, waiting for a response.

"Did you know that when I was fifteen, I used to drink this slush with vodka in it?" I say.

"Don't start on me," Arthur says.

We're in the middle of the summer bake. By noon it's hot, maybe eighty-five, a good day for business. When I pulled out of the garage, Arthur still had the radio on full-roar, waiting for up-to-the-minute weather forecasts. It's the start of a three-day spell, but he still gets nervous, like there's going to be a freak snowstorm or something. In the truck, I open it up on the parkway then hit some familiar sidestreets looking for action, and when there's none, I cut back across the parkway and head down toward a park where some of the kids play baseball.

What Mr. Slush loves is the little ones, tugging at their mothers' hands. I love the way these young mothers smile at this, and you can tell when they're connecting back with their own childhood. But the older kids, the ones with the crumpled dollar bills shoved deep in the cruddy recesses of their pockets, that's where the profit is. They go for Jumbos, sometimes two, and on a hot day like this, I can keep dishing for an hour.

Unfortunately, you put up with some, too. They've heard my music, and I can see up ahead that they've dropped their bats and gloves and sauntered to the curb. They don't want to actually seem like they care, despite whatever left-over childhood excitement churns inside their thorny little hearts.

When I come to a complete stop, they press in. The third kid in line, crew-cut and flushed from the ballgame, leers at me.

"So Mr. Slush," he says. "You too stupid to get a real job, or what?" The other kids suppress giggles. I just grin.

"No," I say, "It's much more complicated than that."

"Yeah?" the kid says. "Like what?"

"It's got to do with probation," I say. "You know, felony charges."

The kids sort of look at each other. I know they think I'm lying; what's funny is that ever since I got out, I've set my mind to truthfulness.

"The chances of me committing an assault again are about nil," I say.

"Yeah, Mr. Slush," the kid says. "Right."

They test you. It's part of being that age. One kid comes up to the window trying to trade me dirty magazines for a cup of slush. Another asks me if he can run a tab. Rule One, I say, wagging my finger. Rule One.

Mr. Slush tries to help them.

"You know, kids," I say, leaning on my elbows, "It's not a good thing to get too hooked on anything, including this slush. What if I gave you freebies, until you got so dependent you couldn't live without the stuff? What if this slush was spiked with a powerful but tasteless narcotic? How do you think Coca-Cola did it? People have powerful designs. I mean, you know nothing about me, really. You don't know what I'd do."

"Like Halloween where they put pins in candy," a dirty faced girl says.

"Sort of," I say. "But imagine that the addiction isn't chemical — just psychological. Are you with me?"

There are four of them, and they just stand there looking at me. Like, Duh.

"Never mind, kids," I say. "Mr. Slush has to push on."

Mr. Slush is trying to make a social contribution. Later in the day, when I come across some kids torturing a cat at the edge of a field, I stop the truck and begin hurling scoops of the product at them, which technically doesn't break any of Arthur's rules. "Stop it! Little demons!" I scream. They squeal and scatter. The cat, which they had with a twine noose around its neck like a chokechain, goes up a tree. "I'll be back!" I shout. Listen, I wish someone had hurled slush at me when I was a kid. I know what they were doing to that cat.

When I come home from work, through the front door of the house, my parents are always sitting in the living room, and I always catch them beginning to stand up, like they've heard an explosion on the street. Their eyes are wide, the look of chronic fright. When I say, "It's just me," I think to myself, "But that's the point, isn't it?" I robbed them blind, even helped steal their car. And while that's one they don't know about, the stuff they do know is reason enough that I shouldn't be living in their house. But they let me, and I'm grateful. I leave my paychecks in a bowl in the kitchen, endorsed, but my folks won't take them, and they accumulate. I eat something I make myself, usually various types of fruits and vegetables. My doctor told me they have a cleansing effect, that I must purge the toxins. After I eat, I tell my folks I'm tired, which I'm usually not, and I go to my room. It's all cleaned out. The accumulated stuff from before — the posters, the old schoolbooks, the magazines and ticket stubs from concerts — are all gone. I threw it all away the first time back, a session of shredded paper and overstuffed garbage bags and muffled obscenities that I think was meant to show Mom and Dad how I was rejecting my frightful past; halfway through I realized I was in a state, and scaring them.

These days, after dinner, I shut the door, strip down to my

underwear, and lie on the bed. I don't have a TV, which is a shame in some ways but another sign of my monk-like self-restraint. I put the radio on soft and just try to be still. I watch the clock, and every time I do I tell myself not to: As each hour approaches, I'm taking deeper breaths. I tell myself I'm that much closer to sleeping, but still I'm struggling along. This is the worst time, when that old itch needs to be scratched. My throat begins to feel dry, but I fight the urge to come out, to go to the kitchen and put my head in the sink and drink from the rushing faucet. This is the time the room seems hot and stifling, even with the window open, even with the sounds from outside coming in. I force my eyes to close and I tell myself the body is a temple, it is a temple. I twitch, I groan. My body is a temple. It's 9:21. The red numerals of my digital clock burn in the dark. Mr. Slush collects himself, feels the damp sheet on his back, and waits for 9:22. Then, somehow, he is asleep.

Walking to the garage at seven in the morning, I'm sweating, and I know that Arthur is going to be insanely happy. It's a ninety-ninety day. That's degrees and percent humidity. Arthur lives for his ninety-nineties, and I tell him he needs to introduce Mr. Slush to Micronesia. "As if nobody else has," he says. I'll be dealing slush like there's no end, and I'll be suffering. But my suffering makes Arthur happy.

In the shady back of the garage, Arthur is loading in ice blocks with one of the kids, Becky.

"Hey," Arthur says, spotting me. "Get ready to make me a wealthy man."

"Municipal pool, Quinn Park, Rec Center, in that order," I say.

Arthur makes a motion like he's pulling a slot machine.

"Ching ching!" he says. "Ching ching!"

"I'm dying already," Becky says. "Three weeks left and I'm

back to school."

"With money in your pocket," Arthur says.

Becky is Arthur's favorite employee. I'm Arthur's favorite project. He knows Becky is going to do all right, and that the kid works hard, and that when she's successful she will think back favorably on Arthur. Arthur wants to be thought well of, which is why he took me off Armand's hands and essentially helped Armand get me squared away. When I get together with Armand to check up on things, he tells me he thinks highly of Arthur, and I say I agree, that everybody thinks highly of Arthur.

I get into the freezer for my ice, and Becky comes in behind me. "I'll help," she says. "I'm done with mine."

"Thanks, Beck," I say. I'm a little in love with her, but it's hopeless, so I go along just being happy to be part of all this. Sometimes I feel like Arthur's my Dad, like Becky's my sister. My real sister, Helen, hasn't talked to me since I got caught with the folks' home entertainment center in the trunk of a buddy's car, in front of a pawn shop. She makes my folks come to her house for visits, and I think she devotes a lot of time to persuading them to cut me loose. Helen looks out for them, and that's a good thing. But if Becky were my real sister she'd forgive me, I think.

And Becky's a strong girl, too: while I'm trying my best with the ice, she pretty much loads the thing up for me. "There you go, champ," she says. "Ready for the road."

"What's your plan?" I say.

"Residentials," she says. "My regulars will be out today. I'll have to take you someday before I go, so they know you for the fall."

Kevin and Shane have come in now, and it won't be long before Arthur reemerges from his office and has us line up for morning instructions. In his office, Arthur keeps a police scanner going, so he can listen for fires. There's nothing like a crowd watching a burning building, for selling slush. Arthur encourages us to watch the sky for smoke. In the event of such a scene, we allow an exception to Rule One: The firefighters get all they want, gratis.

Usually, when Arthur lines us up in the morning, there's nothing much to be said. I think it gives him an excuse to hear all four trucks starting up in one smoky roar.

"Are we prepared to fan out over this parched landscape?" Arthur says.

"I wish I were heading for the beach," Kevin says.

"Head for the beach, then," Arthur says. "But never abandon your post."

"That defeats the purpose," Kevin says.

As we turn to our vehicles, Arthur motions to me. "In my office," he says.

Inside, he lays into me.

"What's this about Nazis in space? I'm hearing stories about Nazis. In space, is that right?"

I can't help smiling. "Where did you hear about that?"

"Where did I hear? My answering machine is full of complaining parents."

"I was simply pointing out an irony," I say, "that the recorded voice on the Voyager space probe contains a tape-recorded greeting to beings of other worlds, and that voice is ex-Nazi Kurt Waldheim, of the United Nations."

Arthur's gaze narrows. "You represent me," he says. "Out there you are Mr. Slush. You're scaring these kids."

"I'm sorry you're mad," I say.

"You don't want to screw this up," he says. "Like I said before, you don't need to talk to the kids. Don't say anything. When they give you trouble, you just pretend like you didn't hear them."

"I understand now," I say. "Like Kurt Waldheim, I can become a more respectable person."

"Starting now," Arthur says.

"Instantaneously," I say.

Out on the road, I keep moving, because the rushing air cools me off. A couple of junior-high boys on undersized bicycles are in the side of the road, waving. I ease up and they step in right in my path.

"Back off!" I yell. "Back off!" Rule Two, Rule Two.

They're reaching over at the counter. "Hands off the equipment," I say.

One kid is this dim bulb with his gut hanging over his belt and a helmet on. The other one is skinny and red-haired.

"So what do you want?" I say.

"Jumbo raspberry," the fat kid says.

I fill the cup and reach out, and he brings up his hand too fast, and the cup goes over. Slush spills all over, dripping red down the white exterior of the truck.

"Jesus!" I say.

The kid watches me mop it up. "Hey, Mr. Slush, are you just a complete screw-up, or what?"

"Pretty much," I mumble.

The red-haired kid turns to the fat one.

"Hey, lay off," he says.

"Shove it," the fat kid says.

"You shove it."

The fat kid looks at him, turns, and saunters off.

"Pisshead," he says.

"Klutz," I say.

"Assface," he says.

The red-haired kid shakes his head.

"Hey Mr. Slush, nobody should talk to you like that. Nobody!" The kid actually looks indignant.

"That Jumbo would have cost a buck and a half," I say.

The kid turns toward his friend, who's picked up his bike and is pedaling away. "Vermin!" he yells.

It could have been my fault, the spill. But it feels nice being defended. I fill another Jumbo and hand it to the skinny kid. "Here," I say. "Thanks."

"Mr. Slush," the kid says, "You're OK."

Later, I'm cruising Parkway, and I see the two of them on a bus bench, sharing said Jumbo. I slow down going by.

"Good work," I yell. "Really great."

"Chump," the skinny kid yells.

On one hand I admire the effort, but all the same I feel guilty.

Rule One, Rule One. I find myself hoping that Arthur doesn't ask me what rules I've broken. He asks me that sometimes. I've made a vow of truthfulness, yet I don't want to have to endure his pouting. I take a buck and a half from my pocket and put it in the register, but I know that doesn't make it right.

I swing left and then left again, and I'm heading for Quinn Park. Some big sales will salve my guilt, I think. I can't squander a ninety-ninety, worrying.

But when I get there, I begin to panic. I've been beaten to the punch by a truck from Ice Cream Castle, which will cut into sales. The girl in the truck nods at me, and I nod back. Mr. Slush still has his devotees, who have waited patiently, but I had wanted to lose myself in a big flurry. But I only take ten minutes filling my orders, and I'm driving again.

I circle by the South Towers but don't stop. I have learned not to waste my time. The Towers are not unfamiliar terrain, my having visited there in a former life to procure certain controlled substances. But the kids, they play on the grassless grounds and don't have a nickel among a dozen of them. Besides, I have fears, of what would happen if I felt the familiar crunch of my tires across that glass-strewn parking lot.

Into the nicer neighborhoods nearby. At a corner, a woman and a little girl.

"Pick what you want, honey," the woman says. She smiles at me and I smile back. I give the child a Pixie, and tell the mother it's seventy-five cents. She smiles. "Let me run in the house," she says. "You caught me without my wallet."

They go around the back of the house and I sit on the counter. I remember when the ice-cream man came by my own house, and how my mother would treat me to little things like this. For a while there, after I became clean, she used to ask me to tell her what it was she did wrong. I said I didn't know, and that she shouldn't ask. My own suspicion is that some people just become screw-ups. It's not psychological, this theory, but it's my actual experience.

"Pop Goes The Weasel" is getting on my nerves, so I cut the sound. After a while, I stand again. Somewhere along there, I realize I'm being stiffed.

I go to the front door of the house and start banging.

"You owe me," I shout. "You owe me!"

In these nicer neighborhoods, police response is amazingly fast. The police cruiser comes at a good clip, pulls in, and the lights stay going. The cop gets out of the car, and I see it's Officer Steve. He is a friend of mine, and of my lawyer's. Officer Steve, when he testified about my misdeeds, had nevertheless expressed a genuine concern for my future, which he didn't have to do. I think that helped.

"What the hell's going on?" Officer Steve says, in a not-alto-gether-unfriendly way. I explain, and he stands nodding. We go to the door together and ring the bell. Officer Steve steps back and shouts to the open upstairs window, "Police, ma'am." The front door opens, and this woman at the door must be eighty years old. She tells Officer Steve that she lives alone, and when we walk around to the back, we see it's easy to go through to the adjoining street.

I come back around and apologize to the woman, and once again Officer Steve speaks on my behalf. On the street, he says,

"If you see them, call me. Don't try to settle it yourself."

"Okay," I say.

"How's Arthur?" he says.

"Arthur is well," I say.

"Arthur is a hell of a guy," Officer Steve says.

Rule One, Rule One. The problem with Mr. Slush, at least in his past life, was the idea of all or nothing. If one has a drink, why not ten? If one is going to take something not his, why not much? Mr. Slush's vow of truthfulness must remain unsullied, lest it all collapse.

I should head for the Rec Center, which is north, but I find myself moving back toward South Towers. Where else would the woman and the child have come from? I will call Officer Steve, should I spot them. In the parking lot, I get out, looking, and I see the first wave of kids coming around the bend. In two minutes, there must be thirty of them, and they just stand there looking at me, and I check every one of their faces, looking for that one girl. None of them say a word, they just look.

"Any of you have money?" I say. None of them say anything. Of course not. "If you don't have money, I can't give you any," I say. "I'm not allowed."

I should go, but I don't. I pull the door of the truck shut and walk across the parking lot, toward the buildings. I'm just looking. There's a playground in the central area, between the buildings, and if the woman and girl aren't there, I'll leave. In the walkway between Buildings One and Two, I brush by some older kids, who may, for all I know, be seeking the goodies I once did.

It's been a while, I see, since I've been here. The playground is gone. There's just an open area now. I go farther, seeing if the playground has been moved. Or perhaps my memory fails me. But in five minutes of looking, nothing turns up. I head back to the truck, where these kids have it circled like they're not going to let me go. I unlock the door, jump up into the seat, and shout for them to get back. They don't. I know the roar of the engine will part them. But when I turn the key, nothing happens.

Mr. Slush is in a fix. In moments like this, Kurt Waldheim's turnaround seems particularly amazing. I keep torquing the key, as if something will now right itself. After becoming accustomed to the silence of the engine, I realize the cooler is no longer humming, as it must, as it truly must.

I am a man stranded in a vessel of melting slush, and I now know I am utterly alone. Even when Officer Steve arrested me that day in front of the pawn shop, I had an accomplice, whom by court order I am allowed no further contact. Even at the defendant's table, Armand was with me. But now, in the hot sun, with a ninety-ninety and no better than five dollars in the till, I see that I am finished.

The children are staring at me.

"Who did it?" I say. "Did you see who did it?" I open the hood and, of course, the battery cables hang like wilted stems.

Back in the truck, I begin filling the cups. I line them up on the narrow shelf, then along the floor and dashboard. When my allotment of sixty cups is gone, filled with melt, I jump down onto the pavement.

"Knock yourselves out," I say. "Go ahead, if it makes you happy." Slush for the needy, I tell myself. It was going to melt anyway. After I've walked a quarter-mile, I look back and see that they are watching me. I get out on Parkway, loping along. It's a good four miles to the ramp of the interstate. I am in flight.

But Mr. Slush lacks the fitness he knew as a boy. The body is a temple, but it is yet under renovation. I find a bus bench under an overhanging branch, and I rest for a long time.

I wish I had sucked down one slush, one bit of sustenance

for my long journey. I have been striving for truthfulness, and the only reality I can admit now is that I have failed once more. But who will mind? My parents will wait through the night and into tomorrow, and then they'll call Helen, who will call Armand, who will call my probation officer, Larry. Officer Steve will be among those notified. With regret and anger, he will look for me.

And where will I go? I'm not sure. What will I do? Not even a clue. I sit for a half an hour, one last pause before becoming a parole violator. I stare and sweat. I gather my strength.

Then, on the road before the bus bench, a car slows, then pulls in front of me. It's a silver Olds, which I realize is Arthur's.

He brings the window down. I see him now, cool in the car, waiting for me to say something.

"How did you know I was here?" I say.

"Get in," he says.

The car is even cooler than I thought, the air conditioner blowing full blast.

"I didn't think you'd find me."

"I heard something on my scanner and came out to look," he said. "Where's the truck?"

"I had some trouble and I was coming to find you," I say. "I was looking for a phone, but I didn't bring any change."

"Yeah, OK," Arthur says.

"I figured if I could get back to the garage. I was panicking."

"Easy," Arthur says. "I know what's going on."

"They stole the battery on the truck."

"It's happened before. These are expensive batteries."

It's a ninety-ninety, but it's begun to turn. The sky has darkened considerably, and as we drive toward South Towers there's a plop of water on the windshield, and then another, and then it just comes down.

It's raining so hard by the time we get there that we can only park and wait it out. Arthur leaves the radio on, playing big-band music, and I look out at the torrent. The truck is washed clean, and I suddenly realize that all the cups are gone. I don't know if the kids took the stuff, or whether the cups have just washed away in the storm.

And then, as suddenly, the rain tapers and dies. We sit, watching mist rise off the pavement, then Arthur gets out, goes to his trunk, and retrieves a tow chain. He loops it around the front bumper of the truck, then to the trailer hitch in the back of his car.

While I'm standing there watching Arthur doing this, a kid rides over on a crappy bike. He looks at me and says, "If you give me a slush, I can show you who took what you're looking for."

Arthur straightens up and looks at the kid. "Screw. Mr. Slush don't make deals."

"Screw yourself," the kid says, and pedals off.

Arthur looks at me. "If we made that kind of deal, do you think we'd really find what we're looking for?"

I shrug.

"We wouldn't," Arthur says. "This is one of many things you'll have to learn. Stick with Mr. Slush, and you will learn these things."

"I will," I say.

"A lesson already," he says. "And it was only worth the price of a single battery."

"I'll pay for it out of my savings," I say.

"You will indeed, and neither of us will mind," he says.

He has me get in the truck and steer, while he tows with the big Olds. Out on Parkway, and then to North, we're moving right along. The wind swirls around me, cooler now, and when I feather the brake to control my speed, I can hear the oscillation of rolling waves of liquid in the cooler. It can be replaced. We drive on. In the opposite lane, another Mr. Slush truck passes by, and I see that it's Becky, looking puzzled. I wave, but she's already past us. We're heading to home base. I am crippled and without power, but I am moving.

The Anchor and Me

The anchor calls me from the road, although I don't know she's on the road until she tells me. The cell phone goes wherever she goes, and as I lie on our living-room couch she informs me that they're doing a remote tonight to lead the Eleven. The anchor hates remotes; the station is doing more to sell her "grit" with prime-time cut-ins and billboards. It's sweeps week and the station wants to show that the anchor can get her makeup to get a little smudged, her hair a bit windblown. They need to prove that she cares that much. Let it be known the anchor strongly prefers the icebox glare of the Newsplex.

In a stroke of luck, tonight's top story is an out-of-the-ordinary murder-suicide. The anchor will lead the Eleven from the victims' front yard, white with lightstands, with the milling, pensive authorities scattered in the rear of the shot.

"Don't worry, I've eaten," the anchor is saying to me, and I hear the cameraman, Lars, chuckle from the driver's seat. These new cell phones pick up everything, and I strongly suspect they've done a hit-and-run at a Chinese place. This is old-home week with Lars, who sulked when she first got put on the Anchor Desk, and who's now all excited, being on the road with her again. It's nine-thirty, nearly the end of my day. But the anchor is just getting pumped, ready for the stand-up.

"So who were these people?" I say.

"He was a beancounter for a big bank downtown," the anchor says. I am a beancounter myself, so I ask the deceased's name. It's nobody I know.

"She was a socialite and do-gooder," the anchor says. "Incredibly photogenic, Thank God. But all we have is piano-top pictures, and Channel 7 supposedly has file video from some charity ball." The anchor makes a wistful sound. "Kelly better come up with something good," the anchor says, half to me and half to Lars.

I think of Kelly now: She's the anchor's serf-like producer who, as we speak, is probably running around begging people to do a top-of-the-hour live shot. Kelly, like all the other producers at the station, considers these her stories. Once, drunk at a station office party, she bitterly confided to me that she considers the on-camera "talent" to be "redundant systems." I wasn't sure how she expected me to respond.

"So are you going to watch?" the anchor says over the roar of the NewsUnit's big engine.

"I'll sure try," I say.

In the morning, when I get ready for work, I can only make out the anchor's burrowed shape under heaps of comforters. The anchor's faux-blond hair, always so carefully done on-air, lies snarled along the edge of the bedding like road-kill. I always feel oddly off-synch dressing myself at six-thirty in the morning, as the anchor regenerates. Our days have become defined by the Six and the Eleven. The anchor has said her life feels the most real when she is on the air. That realness only hit me once: I was walking through a Sears at ten minutes past six one night, heading for the Hardware section, and as I came around a corner and into Electronics, there were a hundred televisions simultaneously pumping out an image of the anchor, a hundred versions of that smile I have come to know so well. I was nearly moved by her omniscience. She is the second-highest-paid talent at the number-one station in the thirteenth-largest market in the most powerful nation on Earth.

My work has nothing to do with any of that. I just made senior investment analyst, a job you do alone in a small room. I make clients happy by telling them when to get in the market and when to get out, and sometimes I save them from ruin. But it seems that when I'm having lunch with my clients, they always come around to asking me about the anchor. They wonder if she's "as nice as she seems on TV." I say, "Of course." I am often introduced as the anchor's husband, with my own name somehow forgotten. I see the flicker of recognition in their faces, and then the excitement. Hey, who doesn't like the anchor? She's got Q-ratings that prove exactly how much.

During the late morning, the anchor calls my office from our bed, checking in.

"Did you see it?" she says, and when I hesitate she says, "Yeah, yeah, yeah..."

"Sorry," I say. "I couldn't keep my eyes open. Too much going on at work right now." She says nothing. "Was it good?" I say.

"It was awesome!" the anchor says. "We had the twenty-year-old son right at the top. He was giving us everything: scandal, adultering, obsession. He said the father was in a jealous rage. He said the mother had tried to get out. The son was really cute, too, which didn't hurt one bit."

"So I guess you owe Kelly," I say.

"Hey, it's Kelly's goddamned job," the anchor says. "Besides, the son specifically asked to be on with me."

"How was he, emotionally?"

"He was in a state of shock, of course, but he still hit all his points," the anchor says. "Dinner after the Six?"

"Dinner after the Six," I say, as always.

When my mother calls a bit before lunchtime, she only wants to talk about last night's Eleven. She's like a groupie when it comes to the anchor, and during sweeps she's nearly out of her mind. I have three brothers, but my mother calls the anchor her "fifth child."

"Did you see her?" my mother says. "She was fabulous!"

"I kind of fell asleep," I say.

"Oh, Les!"

"I'm in the middle of a big project, Mom, remember? I can't watch that late every single night."

"She had the son on," my mother says. "She was incredibly sympathetic to him. That woman just exudes sympathy."

"How's Dad doing?" I say.

"He's reading about it in the paper," she says. "He fell asleep, too."

The anchor and I are both a bit past thirty. We met at a lupus telethon at which she was emcee. How we hit it off is one of those chemical accidents, not unlike the invention of Silly Putty. She was almost nobody then, doing the weekend weather. I was working a phone under the duress of my boss, who had decided the company should get involved. The anchor was co-hosting it with the old guy she'd eventually be teamed with on the Six and Eleven. The anchor and Lars refer to him as "Radio Bob." There had been a time when Radio Bob seemed to have rocklike stability, the Six and Eleven his and his alone. Then the anchor made her move. But that night she was still a comer and it was apparently a big deal for her to be on a local lupus telethon. I went out in the station lobby for some air, and she was smoking furiously, and then licking her teeth.

I've become used to the teeth-licking thing. It's a necessary part of the profession. If she hadn't learned to lick stray lipstick off her teeth, she'd still be sitting on the weekend desk in Green Bay, she says. If she wasn't the type to remember to check her look in the glass lens shield of the videocam, she wouldn't have just gotten a contract extension. "Go ahead, make fun of me," she sometimes says, but she's studied the great ones to understand makeup, and facial gestures, and the almost imperceptible ways an anchor sends out signals. It's obviously gotten her where she wants to be, almost.

Five nights a week, I have the run of the house. Unless I stay in town for dinner with clients or business friends, I come home, make myself something to eat, watch a ball game, and do some work. The house is big, with whole rooms unfurnished until the anchor can consult a decorator.

After the Eleven, she goes to her health club to do stairs and tanning and a swim. Sometimes she gets home at two or three, sometimes later. She operates on almost no food and very little sleep. On weekends, there are always functions she's been asked to, and she never tires of the appearances. Sometimes she sleeps three hours and then does some charity breakfast, followed by a luncheon, followed by a bout of power shopping. For all the space in our big house, there's one couch I pretty much live on.

Thursdays, I join her for dinner after the Six. It's our routine, and I look forward to it. The anchor says getting that far into the week doing the Six with Radio Bob requires a reward. Tonight she's talking about the Flame Room, which is expensive, and I half-expect something's going on: A celebration of last night's coup? A performance bonus? The anchor says the only thing that's really left for her is the call from a network. It's what she's really been waiting for.

When I began dating the anchor, it was nice to be a part of all the commotion. It was in that stage when people didn't know exactly who she was, but they knew they'd seen her somewhere. She was into the Big Hair thing; then Lars referred to her style as a "Crested Stella," and the look instantly changed. Her new style met Lars's approval — he called it "The Muted Halo" — and her Q went sonic. She associates each discarded hairstyle with a market she has now outgrown.

I'll be going to the restaurant from the office, but at four o'clock I call Mission Control, which is the anchor's rather substantial answering machine. You punch 1 to leave her work-related messages, 2 for her personal messages, 3 for appointments and requests for appearances, and 4 for her beeper. I punch 5 to get my own messages; when I do, I hear the anchor: "Here's one for you," she says, and I hear a Lars-like snickering sound deep in the background. "The son of the murder-suicide called me for a date!" The anchor cracks up then, but it doesn't do much for me either way: Everybody asks the anchor for dates. I'm not exactly a secret. We go out plenty. She says she likes the way I look in a tux, and other women will ask the anchor where she's been hiding me. But the anchor's persona seems to require the sense, as her news director Joel says, that she is "emotionally available" to anybody on the other end of the process. According to Joel, the ideal male anchor should be "the Daddy you never had," but the ideal female anchor should be "the girlfriend you always wanted." Joel has told the anchor never to mention on the air that she is married. Her wedding band goes on a little holder. Another professional breakthrough for the anchor came when she learned to play off Radio Bob's Eisenhower-era basso profundo crosstalk and to shoot a knowing look at the camera, like, I know he's lame, too.

The anchor says she tells me about everybody who asks her

for dates. And I've been issued pictures of the stalkers. The anchor rates them on an obnoxiousness spectrum devised by Lars, 1 being Dustin Hoffman in "The Graduate" and 10 being Freddy Krueger in "Nightmare on Elm Street." The latest is some nineteen-year-old broadcasting major from Syracuse University who keeps calling the house asking for a "personal internship," whatever that may be. The kid has pipes like Paul Robeson. When he calls for her, I say, "Try the fucking station." The kid's rated north of Dustin but south of Pepe LePew.

Dinner is at seven-thirty, but I go ahead and work until quarter of eight because I know that when she enters a restaurant she has to have a buffer of time to do the mingle thing. People expect it. She doesn't want to be one of those celebrities who's nasty and distant in real life.

I haven't seen the Six tonight, even though the anchor bought me one of those little palm-sized TVs for when I work late: the wiring in the building must block the signal. I'm sometimes sorry I miss it. I like watching the anchor when she's on a roll, especially when there's good news she can make her own. And one of my few secrets from her is that I like Radio Bob, too. He reminds me of the father I have, when my father wears a tie.

At the restaurant I see the NewsUnit parked across the way, its ponderous roof-mounted satellite dish rubbing against some low-hanging branches. She's going to be going on another remote, and I know dinner will be a little short. But sweeps week will pass, and we'll go back to normal; inside, I bump into Lars, who's coming out of the men's room.

"Oh," I say.

"Kenneth, what's the frequency?" Lars says.

"What are you doing here?" I say.

"Big night," he says. "Busy night."

I follow Lars to the table, where the anchor is sitting at the center of the banquette seat. Lars and I slide in on either side of her. "Les, honey," she says, "we're going to kick some butt tonight."

"How so?" I say.

The anchor leans in conspiratorially. "The son. He's confessing to the double murder! He tipped us through his lawyer, in exchange for our reading the full statement. It's an exclusive. Even the cops don't know yet. He'll turn himself in minutes after I finish."

"This is huge," Lars says. "This is awesome. Sweeps week hall of fame. You cannot fabricate a better story than this for ratings period."

"Les," the anchor says, "Lars just heard a rumor that ABC called and asked for all of this week's tapes. I think this may be the big moment."

"I hear they're looking for a co-anchor to go with Jennings," Lars says.

"Oh, get out of town!" the anchor says.

"Yeah, do," I say to Lars, smiling.

"Hey, pardon me," he says. "Why don't I just eat in the NewsUnit?"

"The Newshog," the anchor says.

"The Newsabago," Lars says. "I should just sit out with Kelly and tear at raw meat."

"Kelly's out there?" I say.

"She's on the phone, getting things lined up," the anchor says. "We'll bring her something in a bag."

When I get home, I stay up and watch the Eleven, making up for last night's transgression. The anchor starts the newscast standing windblown in front of the house, reading the statement from the son, detailing how he fit the hot gun in his dead father's curling fingers, and then told lies about the father's supposed jealousy. "My father was not a jealous man at all..." the anchor reads from the paper. The statement hints that all was not happy in that home, which I suppose didn't even need to be said. I think of that guy, calling the anchor for a date. They show the day-old file tape of him hitting his points with a shaky voice, the anchor clutching his elbow and holding the mike to him. He's a good-looking guy, but I remind myself that he just murdered his parents. I pop the channels, checking the competition. No one seems to have it. The anchor has herself a genuine coup.

I think of the network thing. If it happens, I'd be expected to leave my job. I knew that was possible when we married. Lately, I've been thinking of our life, and about children. The day before we got married, the anchor said she wanted children as soon as she got "established." I've learned what a fluid concept that is. When there's talk of network jobs I begin to wonder if we shouldn't get a move on, childwise.

At midnight, I'm still awake, and I am at twelve-thirty, and for the first time in a long time I think I'll be up when she comes in. But when I awaken, my clock is pulsing and the dawn sky is just bluing and the anchor shifts under the covers next to me. I reach over and touch the small of her back, and whisper, "Time to get started on that baby?"

"Die, hornboy, die," the anchor groans.

On days after the anchor finds herself in a big moment, I myself bask in a reflected glow. I walk in my office and our secretary, Donna, who's talking into her headpiece, gives me the big thumbs up as I find my way to the coffee.

My boss, Chet, calls me at my desk.

"Now that was good shit," he says, and it is an expectation, a correct one, that I know what he's talking about.

"She did well," I say.

"Unbelievable," Chet says. "I sat there watching and couldn't believe it."

"I did, too," I say.

It's Friday night, and I've worked late just to get out in front of things, and it feels okay not to have to rush through it. Working on a Friday night in the empty office isn't so bad a feeling, I've found. Solitude suits me, and I suppose in that way the anchor and I have a complementary life. Getting home, it's maybe a little after ten; I hang the dry cleaning on a doorknob, grab a beer and flop on the couch to wait for the Eleven.

At 11:00:01 p.m., as the rising orchestral NewsCenter theme commences and the klieglights come up on the gleaming Newsplex, I can see that Radio Bob is alone at the Newsdesk, and I wonder where they've dispatched the anchor now. It's the last night of sweeps; I know that despite her successes the anchor will be glad to come in from the cold. Radio Bob introduces the top story in that low rumble of his that reminds me of gathering thunder; and then in a cut we see the anchor at a broad intersection in a nondescript suburban pocket, where there has been a head-on collision. A quad-fatal, with four more being airlifted to local hospitals. And the anchor, looking grave and concerned and giving her head that weighted tilt that she got from Diane Sawyer, begins to relate the details. She says that alcohol could be a factor, and she says a city is in mourning. She says incidents like this remind us of the fragility of life. It happened in front of a crowded bus stop, she intones, and many witnessed the carnage, and will be referred to counseling. Then she reaches beyond the border of her shot and pulls a fat bearded guy on-camera with her, identifying him as an eyewitness.

When she prompts him, the guy leans in and says, "Bob, the

afternoon stillness of the quiet Edgewood section of the city was shattered today..." I sit up straighter. This doesn't sound quite right.

"Yes, shock and sadness are the emotions on what was an ordinary evening in a local neighborhood..."

The guy's hijacking her stand-up. He is talking in Televisionese, and he is a gifted mimic; the incongruity of him out of his prescribed role is a shock and a parody.

"The moan of metal and the shattering of glass pierced the calm around 8:15 p.m.," the bearded guy goes on. I see the anchor's profile frozen in terror: Eyewitnesses are supposed to describe what they saw "in their own words," with all its stammering and grammatical gaffes. But he is sounding uncannily like ... the anchor.

She's going to have to cut him off. But containment is not the anchor's strong suit. In fact, the anchor is lost outside of her tightly scripted realities, something she knows but still doesn't want to admit. She begins to turn toward the camera, to do the eye contact thing. But then she jerks her head back as if she realizes that her look would hold nothing but fear. The bearded guy, smooth and not half-bad except for foodstains on his shirt, has already reached up and put his hand over hers, applying equivalent tension to the mike so that she can't get it away unless she starts wrestling him. I say, aloud, "No!" The anchor is being upstaged and has lost control. Her Q is flying around like a deflating balloon and her only out is for Lars to yank a wire and go to static — but he's behind the camera as we all are and we can only watch and for all I know Lars secretly enjoys it. Kelly must be there, too — she must have found this bearded guy and told the anchor to bring him on, and she will pay for it.

"Enough," the anchor says now. "Okay, that's enough!"

The bearded guy looks at her, then into the camera, and says, "A full inquiry will follow." The anchor can only swallow and say, "Bob…"

Back in the Newsplex, Radio Bob is merciless. He looks into the camera and does a Jack Benny take that seems about twenty minutes long but is probably only three seconds, and I hoot out loud. "And in other news," he says ponderously.

I don't bother watching the rest. The anchor will be back on to lead in some other stories, but I've seen all I need to see. ABC's omniscience hangs all over things, like a mist.

When the anchor crawls into bed, I look at the clock. It's two-thirty. I shift a little, and tell her hello. Her hair is damp, smelling of chlorine from the health club pool.

"I've been thinking I want to buy a new car," the anchor says.

"Don't need a new car," I say.

"You'd look good in a new car," she says.

"I look good enough," I say.

"Hmmm," she says.

"We should really think about having that baby," I say now.

"Maybe," she says. "I don't know."

We lie there in bed and I think of that. The anchor shifts, trying to get comfortable.

"That damned Kelly," she says. "She ought to be fired."

"How about Lars, too?" I say. "He's the one I'd love to see go."

She half-turns toward me, surprised.

"Jealous," she says.

"No."

The anchor gives a little giggle, the grating sinus-involved giggle that nearly sank her in Green Bay when she let it slip on the air. She overcame that, too. The voice lessons gave her a husky suggestive laugh, but that's one I don't hear off the TV.

"Go to sleep," I say, but she is already back with her own thoughts.

I relax, and with the anchor there beside me I begin to doze again. At 3:56 I awaken, alone in bed. I hear a sliding sound and realize it's her, in the walk-in closet, putting on her running clothes.

"God," I say.

"Just a couple of miles," she says. "I won't really be that long."

The door slams, and I am alone again. The anchor will meet the day puffing down avenues and side streets, even through people's yards if she needs to. People who catch her doing that can brag about whom they spotted cutting across the lawn. It's early, though, and Saturday. Only once in a while, she'll see someone, or maybe a dog. But I guess I shouldn't worry about her out there. She's armed with one of those little cans of pepper gas. And I know she's ready to use it if something gets in her way.

What I Have Noticed

I awaken early now. I become conscious of the darkness and I pull myself up to a sitting position at the edge of the bed. After a while, I put on my slippers; when I go to the kitchen, I see the green glow of the clock on the microwave oven, and it is always within minutes of five. I don't keep a clock in the room where I sleep. The pattern of rest and wakefulness, over these many years, has become finely calibrated.

I am a doctor fast approaching the age at which I should retire, and there are those nights, of course, when I have evening rounds at the hospital, or when I am on call. At home, on call, I'll watch a game on television, with an outdated prescription pad next to me for making notes. I fall asleep; the phone rings and I pitch forward, instantly lucid. I realize now that this is the product of my medical-school training, something that has stayed with me even as I age: I am past sixty years old and I can still awaken at two in the morning to dispense clear and correct instructions to a worried parent. I remain dressed on those nights I sit up, not wanting to be too comfortable. After I take a call, I am back asleep before I can finish putting the pen away. In the morning, my wife finds my shirts with tiny blue ink trails descending into my breast pocket.

These stains, she removes. I wear white shirts those nights so she can use strong bleach. She could send them out to be cleaned, but this has become our arrangement, just as it has that when I come to the kitchen at five in the morning, the coffee is ready. The coffee maker has been filled the night before, the timer set for a quarter to five. These are a few of the many small favors Ruth and I exchange each day. Years have passed since she's said she loves me, or I have said I love her, but in the evening, when I hear the coffee grinder going in the kitchen, I remind myself that a string of words is no more precise an expression than a small and prosaic action. An example: As a pediatrician, I have sometimes been called as a witness in child-abuse cases. When I am called, I simply attest to the bruises and cuts. I try to be truthful about what I have witnessed. I am often asked how I can be so sure that the injuries weren't caused by some other reason, if they couldn't have been accidental. I often answer that no one can be absolutely sure of anything. I don't play judge and I don't condemn anyone, because I believe we all have stronger consciences than we would care to admit. But what I have noticed is that in these trials, in which parents are accused of inflicting or allowing horrible pain to their children, that these parents quite often speak of love. What I can say in these instances is that the evidence almost always speaks for itself.

And so, for my wife, I do things. In the morning, I go out on the snowy walk to fetch the morning paper, but I don't read it. Ruth likes a fresh newspaper, which she peels carefully as she moves through it. I listen to the news on my kitchen radio sometimes, although on many days I get along fine with no news at all. I haven't read a book for pleasure in twenty years, which is certainly not a boast. In the evening, I gather my medical journals and go through them again and again. Another thing I do for my wife is sleep in a separate room. Ruth was greatly relieved when I first suggested this, because she didn't want to hurt my feelings. I snore terribly. I also have a mild case of apnea. She has since told me how she'd lie in bed listening for me to start breathing again, waiting in the dark. It jangled her nerves. For a while, we tried to confront it. I slept for a week with a tennis ball sewn in the back tail of my pajama top, for the purpose of forcing me to lie on my side. Asleep, I writhed in my bedclothes, bent on conquering it. It didn't bother me — I wasn't even aware of my struggle. But I could see each morning in Ruth's rheumy eyes that the situation was completely unfair to her. My clothes are still in our bedroom, so it seems as if I haven't really moved out. It's just that when it comes time to sleep, I go across the hall, and shut the door behind me. It was our daughter's room, and it looks much the way it did when she moved away for good, the summer after she graduated from college. It is an adult's room, with the effects of her childhood, the stuffed toys and riding ribbons, put away by her that August.

We had two children. My son lives alone in the city, and on weekends he sometimes comes out. We golf, the two of us, and after our round he comes home for a sandwich, and to see his mother. In the fall he helps me with the storm windows, in the spring with the screens; he drives us to the airport when we travel. He doesn't sleep over, even though we tell him he is welcome. But he calls often, to see that we are fine.

I have been a pediatrician for more than thirty years. Much has changed in the way we treat children, but I have noticed that the most significant change is in what people used to call "bedside manner." When I was young, I spoke to people as fellow parents. I told them I understood the way things weighed on their minds. Now I'm a paternal presence, with my glasses and my whitening hair. To save time for questions is important, but it takes a certain nature to gently signal it is time for me to move on, to other waiting parents. I try not to leave them feeling as if they are alone. Some of my younger colleagues are working on this technique, but they work under much more difficult sets of rules. Twenty years ago, I could tell the parents of a sick child that I thought things would turn out for the best. In a case in which a child was gravely ill, I'd say that there was still much good reason to hope. And this was all the truth, because I am an optimist. But these days, to say that kind of thing is awfully dangerous. I know doctors who've been sued by grieving parents. This is usually a troubling and futile situation. It's as if there's been a breach of contract, and that all contracts now stipulate that sick children will get well, that illness and tragedy has somehow come to be an unnatural contingency. Yet I don't blame the parents. They're in shock, and they lash out. This age we're in does not account for the will of God. Somebody must be blamed.

I tell other doctors that it might be our own fault. "If it feeds our egos to be treated as if we're infallible, then we damn well better be infallible," I say. I've seen too many young doctors who've argued and defended themselves over the tiniest mistakes, because they're so scared of being perceived as human. The nurses in my office seem to like me, and I think it's because I acknowledge and accept their help, something they don't often get from several of the younger associates, who buy expensive cars and drive too fast and invest foolishly in the stock market, believing that medical degrees will carry them through other difficult areas in life.

I've never been so sure. Even when I received my medical degree, I doubted I had extraordinary intelligence. Of course that was a different era, but yet I've never doubted my capabilities as a physician. I still read the medical journals the day they arrive, well before my younger friends. When they sit at staff meetings and talk about new treatments, I will toss in a remark not only to help but to defend myself against their suspicion about old doctors, which is that we rely too much on old methods to float us through the final years. But I still attend medical conferences based on subject matter rather than the proximity to golf courses. I study the handouts in my hotel room while my wife shops and finds restaurants we can enjoy together. We usually stay a few days after the conference has adjourned, so that I can golf on my own time. I'm sure this matters to no one but myself. But still, I sometimes hope someone will notice this habit, and what it means.

Is is vain to worry about what others think? Certainly. But most of us try to keep our vanities modest, I think. I was drawn to medicine as much out of vanity as anything: I wanted to master a difficult art, which brings with it a certain respect, and I still feel the need to be seen as more than simply capable.

Yet the bulk of my work is conducting routine check-ups. The younger doctors here aren't interested in these. I tell them that of every ten sick children we see, nine will get better on their own. We can accelerate healing and alleviate pain, but we effect the final verdict more rarely than we'd admit. But the young doctors have come from lengthy and arduous training. They wait hopefully for the rare and dramatic case. They presume victory. Check-ups bore them.

So I do the check-ups. The younger doctors share knowing looks. I will risk being overly vain when I say that I'm as able as any of them to solve the hard cases; but yes, these check-ups pay bills and build up my retirement account. But there are other reasons. I enjoy the nature of the reassurance. Although there has not been a child in my house in many years, I know the television characters and I can amuse the parents when I lift the stethoscope to a patient's shoulder blades and tell the child I'm listening for funny noises.

"Did you swallow Minnie Mouse?" I say. "Is that a bunny hiding in your ear?" The child's arms, tensed by the coldness of the instrument, will relax; the parents will smile. I will bring on a silence in the room and for a few seconds can receive the vigorous flutter of a growing heart. My ears are sharply tuned: I can tell you stories. The cardiologists have told me more than once that my ears, while not what they used to be, have picked up on ailments that might otherwise have continued undetected. Using the stethoscope, that lowly and proven tool. This is a function of experience. I reaps me many warm Christmas cards each year.

Ruth and I dine out three times a week. I only have one drink now, and I pass up some foods I used to eat, especially the heavy sauces I've always had a taste for. I had a bout with angina a while back, so I try to be more careful. We enjoy these dinners out, and we like to go to places where we might run into friends. We don't associate with many medical people, which is just as well. On those evenings we stay at home, we usually eat light meals, my food set on a tray while I read or take calls from the hospital. Ruth occupies herself in the bedroom or the kitchen. After thirty-five years of marriage, I feel less certain about what my wife is thinking at any given time. This is the acquired wisdom of a long marriage — that I probably know more, but think I know less. I really haven't done anything alone since I was a very young man, but we afford each other a sense of privacy that keeps each of us content.

We used to talk about what each of us would do if the other died. This was when we were in our early fifties, when our children were reaching adulthood yet still dependent on us. But since my chest pains, the talk has stopped. The answer seems more clear, even though neither of us expects anything to happen for quite a few more years. But I know Ruth is prepared if it happens, and that makes me proud of her.

Another thing I've done for her is agree to put away many of the photos we've displayed around the house. The photos are of our daughter, who died two years ago. My wife says she has overcome the grief we each went through; she says, however, that sometimes the pictures can bring on a sadness that can catch us off guard. I don't have those feelings, but I respect Ruth's emotions. We have put all of those pictures together in one place. They are still in their frames, in the bottom drawer of the dresser in the room in which I sleep. The pictures are there for us to look at when we want to. Ruth looks at them more than I.

Our daughter died of cancer. She was thirty-one. At first, Ruth and I depended very much on each other to get through this. I remember the ride to the cemetery, in the limousine. I looked out the window and I saw a young man jogging in the sunlight, as you see people doing on any day of the week. I felt surprised that anyone would be doing something like that on such a day. Then I thought about how ridiculous I was being. How could we complain? Our daughter died as a grown woman, and she fell to the sorts of odds we rationally know exist. People in their thirties die of cancer. What else is there to say? We quietly realized that we're not special. From the outward signs — for parents can probably never truly know — it seems she had a happy life. We were at her side almost until the end; her husband asked us if he could be alone with her when the time came. It seemed like the right thing, to let it happen that way.

My son and I golf almost every Saturday morning, unless there is snow. I know the old joke, about doctors and golf, and I'll admit that as a young man I took up the game because it was the game doctors play, and I was a doctor. At first, I couldn't stand it. The game tested my patience. I'd watch my ball slice slowly into the trees and I'd seethe. Once I threw my driver into a pond. I had a boy caddying. He happened to be a patient of mine, someone to whom I'd recently finished explaining the facts of life, at the request of his mother. In that lecture, I had affected an air of total dispassion. The key to explaining sex to children is to act so unemotional that the child can't possibly think that you've done it yourself (I recommend this approach to parents). But on the golf course that morning, he saw an animal. I caught his stare of disbelief, and that made me laugh, which made him grin. I paid him five dollars to wade in after my driver, and I never lost my temper after that.

Now I'm glad I persevered with the game. I have come to appreciate the arc of the well-hit ball, its silent bounding far up the course, without losing faith in the aftermath of my still-frequent slices. Golf also gives me a chance to be with my son. He was always quiet, and this near-wordless union on the course helps preserve our connection.

When they were children, his sister liked to dress him up like a doll, even with their mother's makeup sometimes, and he always let her. In the office, I witness siblings who beat up on one another, which is common. Early on, I could see that as a parent, I was fortunate. In church, my children would be both quiet and behaved, a walking advertisement for my practice. Although I told parents that such things were often beyond anyone's control, I felt quietly superior.

I always pictured my family as the corners of a square, in perfect proportion to one another. My son would have been the corner across the diagonal, the one slightly more distant. The second child becomes treated as one of a pair, never getting the full attention the firstborn is afforded; he came seven years after her, when I was in the midst of getting a practice off the ground. His mother and sister were always there, though, attending to him.

Now, I try to rethink the geometry. I can see that my son does, too. And Ruth. For a while, with our son and daughter and son-in-law, we envisioned a slowly expanding constellation. We hold such hopes still, because it is logical to assume our son will someday marry and have children. Ruth longs for grandchildren, but we agree it would be unfair to mention this, to burden our son, to enhance any loneliness he might feel. But with our daughter gone, we've lost her husband, too. They had no children, and he apologetically faded away. He's a good man. We reassured him that he had to go out and start fresh.

We try not to pressure our son. We know it takes an effort to come down and see us so regularly. He has a career to think about and it requires long hours. Golf is good, because he and I can fill the hours with talk of the game, and on a nicely played hole we can exult in success without any strings attached. When we eat afterwards, it is always with a rude hunger.

I think there's a reason why I don't look at the pictures in the dresser drawer as often as Ruth does. It has to do with my work, I think.

There was a point, maybe ten years ago, where I was stunned at the recognition of how mechanical things had become. I realized that despite my self-image as a healer, I got up in the morning vaguely fearful of the coming day, for its routine and its repetition. Like most people, it was a phase, but in the last year or so, I've suddenly entered a new phase, in which I seem freshly infatuated with the idea of going to work. I leave early now, just to be there, and I am eager for the rounds of examinations. I come into the examining room, where the child and the parents have been waiting. I go to the child and hold the arms and feel the abdomen, and when I look in the mouth I am gentle with the tongue depressor, doing it slowly so as not to frighten anybody. I feel the strength of small arms against my soft grip. With the infants, I pull them up off their backs and feel their tiny fists clench my fingertips, as they should. I listen to the vigorous flutter of a growing heart, and with sick children I can at least make them feel a little better. The ones who fall very ill must go to specialists; I deeply respect (but don't envy) the doctors who must follow illnesses to the end, day in and day out. The sad moment when I lose a patient is in contrast to the waves of healthy children I hold and lift and wrestle with each day. I have become happy again in that simplest pleasure, telling a mother that her child is perfect.

When I was a young man, my decision to become a pediatrician was an abrupt one. I had gone through the process of ruling out possibilities: I don't have the hands of a surgeon, a revelation that came so early on that there was little disappointment. Specialties that would have brought a stunning income seemed far too narrow, too removed from the lives of my potential patients. In my day, the concept of general practice seemed tired and outdated.

At the time I was deciding, my daughter was an infant, and I have no doubt that this influenced my decision. I was a new parent, and I marveled at her, this small human being. I held her and felt exhilarated at the feeling of her gripping my neck as I sat at night, studying with her wedged in the crook of my arm, calmed by her small breaths.

She grew up, and we have lost her. Each day, I get to feel the children in my doctor's hands, I get to feel these small complex biological systems, systems that will grow and eventually fail, but not for a very long time.

On Sunday mornings, after I've had my coffee, I go to church. I'm not an overly religious man, but I have certain beliefs. I go to seven o'clock Mass, where Father Paul knows this is a golfers' service and keeps things duly expeditious. I will go on for nine holes, and Ruth will go to a later Mass. I can count on her lighting candles for the both of us.

Besides the candle she lights for our daughter, Ruth lights four others, for our parents. Of the four, my father was the last to go. That was more than ten years ago. He was seventy-six, twenty years a widower. He had learned how to be by himself; in those later years, he and I shared something different than we had before. We'd had some rough moments when I was a boy, as I had with each of my children. I recalled that when I found out that my daughter had started smoking. She was fifteen. Ruth and I agonized, but held back from saying anything. I feared that the problem was somehow me. I wasn't home very much, with all my work. When I did speak up, letting my anger spill into what was supposed to be a rational talk, it ended up in a loud argument. I left the house then, to let Ruth try to speak to her, and I went to my father's. He brought out cigars and drinks, and we talked about when he caught me smoking. I argued that I'd been older, in college, and that I'd been smoking cigars, which weren't as bad. He got angry thinking about it, so he reached out at me and rapped his knuckles against my middle-aged forehead. After he died, I lost my taste for cigars.

I sat with my father during the last few days of his life, juggling my schedule so I could be in the hospital where he was. He passed on a February afternoon, the day after a blizzard. The sunlight, amplified by the snow, made the room dazzlingly white. In the last day, my father stepped into a chamber of his memory with which only he was familiar. He looked at the wall past the foot of his bed, and he talked with people whom he must have known. "Where are you going, Billy?" he said to me, and I wondered who Billy was. "Don't be late, Bill," he said. There was, I think, a boy who had lived within his mind for many years, looking out a window for a last time.

In the mornings, when I shave, I look in the mirror and see my father's face. I take stock in myself and tell myself I feel the same as when I was thirty. But my body, at times, tells me differently. The angina, just a brief spell, punctuated that. But I still refuse to believe.

I don't feel particularly fearful about what's ahead. When my father was alive, I'd visit him at his apartment. He had a hard time at first; when my mother died, he sold his house; he and I spent the following weekend throwing out almost everything of hers. I thought he would regret it later, but he never again mentioned that day. But when I'd go to his little apartment, to take him to his doctor or bring him to my house for dinner, he'd fumble for his glasses or walk the edges of rooms trying to find his wallet. "Your mother is playing tricks on me again," he'd say, and it was clear he wasn't joking. He was quite often irritated by her playfulness.

The younger doctors I know find it difficult to resolve the spiritual with the scientific. They speak of studies that make the daily miracle seem less wondrous and stripped of mystery, and they feel a sense of triumph about such findings, as if explaining away the magician's slick illusion. I say that the particulars don't interest me so much, and the significance is not necessarily lost. I read in the newspapers about about the near-death experience, and wonder why these are such a recent phenomena. Are our tools becoming better at reeling back the nearly departed? My daughter and I spoke of this once, of the bright light and the sense of seeing one's demise from a distance. This was when we still thought she'd get better. We talked of how those who had reported the experience would see familiar people, beckoning them to cross the threshold.

As I have said, I am generally an optimistic man. I told my daughter I believed these people to be sane and honest.

Once, when I was younger, I had a patient, a very small girl, who died. She'd been born in terrible shape, with a leaky heart and badly formed limbs. It was only a matter of time, and I was surprised she lasted past the age of two. Afterwards, I went to the wake. I can't always do that, but I try when possible, depending on the situation. The girl's brother, also a patient of mine, sat next to me in one of the folding chairs. He waited for a bit, then turned to me, and I leaned in to him to listen. He must have been four. He wanted to know when she was going to learn to talk. "I think we'll have to wait and see," I said. I recently gave this boy his physical for college. It was his last visit to me. We joked about him, six-foot-three, having to sit in a waiting room with Mother Goose on the walls. He would move on to a new doctor, but I was glad to see him before he left, and I'm sure he doesn't remember what he asked. It would seem to him a different life, childhood. I think of each patient as a series of people. I see them, when they are healthy, at intervals that provide a breathtaking demonstration of how we change and adapt.

Years ago, when I was in my late twenties, I still loved to sleep late, a pleasure I no longer covet. Saturday was the only day I could try. Those mornings, my daughter, a little girl, would awaken and come to the side of the bed. I suppose it is because I am a lighter sleeper than Ruth, or because it was an unusual sight for me to be still sleeping, she would come to my side. She was always a patient child, and I think she must have waited for a while. Then, when she was ready, she'd reach out and touch my bare arm, a silent delicate touch, and I would open my eyes and see her. I'd get out of bed, and we'd go quietly to the kitchen, and I would make toast.

At night, in the room in which I sleep, I sometimes think she's there, the daughter I had three decades ago. In the dark, I sense her at the side of the bed, waiting. At first, I was troubled by this. I wondered why I didn't form visions of the daughter I last knew, the adult. The truth is, I'm having a harder time remembering her face, her grown-up face, as clearly as I'd like. I wanted to think of the child at my bedside as a ghost, and imagined that in its infinite dimensions there are other ghosts, and that while the adult may be off on other visits, that it is the child who will best give me comfort.

I believe in ghosts. I know this is unfashionable, but it is still how I feel. In my sleep, I sometimes think I sense her touching me. But then, awake, I realize it's just the warm edge of the sheet against the skin along my wrist. I also know that each day, I will get to hold a child like she once was. I will listen to the beating heart and perhaps feel a timid child's hot tears, as natural and healthy a sign as anything. In the morning, when I awaken in the dark and see that no one is in the room, when I sit up at the edge of the bed and put on my slippers, I feel well-rested.

Carnegie Mellon University Press
Series in Short Fiction

Friends of
Carnegie Mellon University Press
Series in Short Fiction